Lock Down Publications and Ca$h
Presents

I0670245

TIL
DEATH 2

The Consequence of
Blind Loyalty

Written By
ARYANNA

Lock Down Publications
P.O. Box 944
Stockbridge, GA 30281
www.lockdownpublications.com

Like our page on Facebook: Lock Down Publications
www.facebook.com/lockdownpublications.ldp

Stay Connected with Us!

Text **LOCKDOWN** to 22828 to stay up-to-date with new releases, sneak peaks, contests and more…

Like our page on Facebook:
Lock Down Publications

Join Lock Down Publications/The New Era Reading Group

Visit our website:
www.lockdownpublications.com

Follow us on Instagram:
Lock Down Publications

Email Us: We want to hear from you!

Chapter 1

January 2028
Kentucky

The sounds of numerous insects having their way with the night was somehow soothing as I sat on the balcony smoking a blunt. At first, I'd thought that being out in Kentucky, in the country, would be a difficult adjustment for me, but I was wrong. There was something about the freedom of wide-open spaces that called to both me and Gini, which aided in keeping our minds straight despite all the bullshit. I knew that there would be fallout behind our daring prison break, but not having the foresight of betrayal had left us somewhat unprepared. I never thought that Candice, a woman I'd considered one of my wives and part of my family, would be disloyal by telling the feds that the attack on Fluvana Correctional Center wasn't terrorist motivated. I never thought she would tell them people that I'd declared war on the United States of America just to break my wife out of prison. She did though, and now every law enforcement agency with jurisdiction was asking questions that I didn't need answered.

Gini and I had been hiding out for two weeks so far, and no one knew where we were except for those who were a part of The Nation of Rulers. The problem was that the world wasn't ready to believe that Gini was dead, or that I was out of town on vacation like my lawyer claimed. It was becoming increasingly apparent that the longer I stayed away, the closer everyone was gonna look for the truth in what Candice had alleged. A move had to be made, and that knowledge was what had me sitting on the balcony, alone, at 2 o'clock in the morning with my lungs full of smoke.

My first instinct had been to just keep putting distance between us and the state of Virginia, but the constant news coverage told me that this idea was shortsighted. The people wanted answers, and that public outcry wouldn't vanish with Gini and me, which had forced upon me the indisputable truth. A move had to be made.

"L..." Gini called softly.

I could see her on the king-sized bed in the bedroom we shared, but I didn't go to her. "L..." she called again, but with the sound of need filling her throat.

Still, I didn't move. I just stared at her while continuing to smoke my blunt. The sudden sounds of her moans rode the slight breeze, reaching my ears and causing a familiar tingle in the pit of my stomach.

With every second that passed, I could feel the temptation rising, but I fought against it because work always trumped pleasure. Even as her moans became more insistent, my mind circled back to what needed to be done now, as well as ten moves from now. Being a student of the laws of human nature, I understood the dangers of being shortsighted, but just like anything else, application was different at times. Practice was required until perfection was realized, or I might as well put my gun in my mouth now and bite the bullet.

My analytical mind was telling me that the best move that I could make was to face my accusers head on, but only once I was ready. It was a risky move, but what was life without risk? I was raised in the streets, and from experience, I knew that snitching wasn't some new shit that had just popped up. That shit was trending way before Twitter existed, and there was no way to stop it from spreading. There were ways to make it difficult, and one of those ways was to force a muthafucka to do it in your face. Whispering about me was easy, so I was gonna have to make Candice say it with her muthafuckin' chest!

The hardest part about my next play was that I was gonna have to make it without Gini by my side, and I didn't know how she was gonna take that news. She could understand logic, but our love wasn't logical, and the power that it wielded within us could cause the most unlikely of responses. Somehow, I would have to convince her.

"Oh my God! L! Can I...can I cum?" Gini pleaded.

My eyes and mind shifted back to her in this moment, and I felt a smile tugging at the corners of my mouth. Gini's blue eyes blazed in the darkness, locking on my face, as Dana pushed her widely-spread legs up by her ears so that she could push her tongue deeper inside her.

"Fight it," I demanded before taking a long, lazy pull from my blunt.

"I can't, I can't, baby, she...she-"

"You asked me and I answered you. Don't cum; just fight it," I stated again, smiling devilishly at her. The expression on Gini's face could only be described as annoyed arousal, but it was beautiful.

When Dana switched up the game by moving her tongue to Gini's asshole and pushing two fingers at a fast rhythm inside Gini's pussy, her entire expression shifted. She went from a regular tornado to a sidewinder in seconds, and her moans became breathless grunts of unmistakable pleasure.

"Fight it," I instructed, finally rising and going back into the bedroom. The sight of Dana's big, pretty brown ass tooted up in the air as she was face down in my wife's pussy had me hard and yearning, but I continued to observe.

"Baby, get-h-h-herrrrr," Gini sang out, struggling to keep her eyes from rolling. I knew that she wanted me to level the playing field by fucking Dana good like we'd done before, but I was content to be a spectator in these games.

"Sorry babe, I can't help you this time," I replied, still watching intently.

"You-you pussy!" Gini moaned, holding on tightly to Dana's purple dreadlocks. My laughter echoed off the walls while playing tag with the sounds of pleasure tearing her throat apart. "Leroy, please!" Gini begged.

I waited a few more seconds while polishing off the last of my blunt, and then I gave her a subtle nod. Moments later, her screams grew until the sounds of the nighttime insects were long forgotten. Her body's convulsions would've given any bull rider a run for his money, but Dana stayed in the saddle and rode Gini into submission. Having a threesome was an erotic and sexy thing, but sometimes just watching was sexier.

"You good, champ?" I asked once the shaking had stopped threatening to collapse the huge roof we were under.

"Fuck-fuck you, L. That was cruel," Gini replied, fighting for air.

Dana giggled as she got up off the bed and came to stand in front of me. When I slid my hand to the back of her neck, she reached up to link her arms around my neck and pulled me in for a kiss.

Pussy, desire, and weed was the most interesting and intoxicating combination that I'd ever tasted, and the indulgence of it now threatened to put me in the bed between both women. With great restraint, I pulled back after a moment, but I kept Dana locked within my embrace.

"I've got a plan," I said softly.

"I'm sure it's a good one too. What do you need from me?" Dana asked.

"I need you to keep her safe," I replied, nodding towards my still sexually-disoriented wife.

"You don't even have to ask that, L. So what's the catch?"

"The catch is that I'm going back to Virginia solo, and you two are gonna stay here," I said.

"What?" both women cried in unison.

7

A quick look at Gini told me that she hadn't been too cum-dazed to not be listening, and that afterglow she'd been wearing was now gone. "Before either of you panic, I want you to hear me out first," I said, taking a step back from Dana and holding my hands up to silence them. Neither woman said anything, but their frustration was easy to interpret. "If we keep running with all these unanswered questions and speculation, then it's only a matter of time before we get caught. Even with all the money we have, I doubt that any government will hide us once the United States starts throwing the words Domestic Terrorist around. They damn sure ain't going to war with a superpower for us. So we gotta be smart about this shit, and everybody has to play their part in this."

"I'm gonna need you yo explain that more clearly, Leroy," Gini said, climbing out of bed and standing next to Dana.

"I need to play the role of the grieving widower who wants answers just as bad as law enforcement. Gini, I need you to play dead like you're in an old Western," I stated.

"And what about me?" Dana asked.

"Dana, I need you to be the invisible hand that brings about the fear of God to all those who would think to betray or threaten what Ruler has built. It's universally known that female assassins are more effective because by the time they're viewed to be the actual threat, it's too late. I need your chapter of Rulers to be ready to ride whenever on whoever," I replied.

"I can do that," Dana said without hesitation.

All eyes moved to Gini now because we all understood that her playing dead meant that she had to remain out of sight. This was a blow to her pride, but it was my hope that she would see past that.

"Leroy, I swear to God that I'm gonna fucking kill you if you die," Gini growled between clenched teeth.

"Understood, my love," I said, smiling.

"Well now you DEFINITELY owe us a threesome, so come on," Dana demanded, taking my hand and leading me to the bed.

I didn't resist, but I intended to teach them.

Chapter 2

Lia

I sat there looking at her body, staring into her lifeless eyes, wondering if THAT would be me one day. And that's when I made my decision...

"Lia! Lia, baby, wake up, you're having a nightmare."

The sound of Imani's voice finally pierced the fog and released me from the death grip the past had on my heart. No matter how many times I had this same nightmare, it never dimmed when it came to realism. I still saw my baby sister's body on my living room floor, and I could never forget the man who'd put her there: our very own father.

"I'm good, bae," I said, swinging my feet to the floor so that I could climb out of bed.

I felt Imani's desire to hold me, but she knew I'd never let that happen in this vulnerable moment because I was too gangsta for that. I walked into our bathroom, turned on the hot water, and stepped beneath its overhead cascading flow. My ritual was to stand here until the bag of mixed emotions came and went. Despite being in a solid relationship, it was my belief that my vulnerability was mine and mine alone to deal with. After about 45 minutes, I'd regained my composure enough to turn the water off and step out. Even through the fog of steam surrounding me, I could smell the good weed Imani was smoking in the bedroom. When I stepped back out of the bathroom, she handed me an already lit blunt, and then she headed in the direction of the kitchen.

I sat on the side of our bed, and let the cool breeze pushing through the open window dry my body while I smoked. I detested the weakness in myself because here it was five years after the fact, and I still couldn't get past Cyn's murder. I tried justifying it, rationalizing it, and even went so far as to try and brush it off because she and I hadn't known each other for that long. Nothing worked. The nightmares still came, and with it came the unshakable rage for a father that could harm his own kid. Our father had played God by becoming the devil, and I was forever haunted by that. The only thing that terrified me more was the knowledge that we shared DNA, and some of his evil could right now be pumping through my veins. I hadn't come face to face with it yet, but I was always consciously looking for it.

"Your uniform is in the closet. I'm going to make you some breakfast before you go," Imani said from beyond the bedroom door.

"I'm not hungry, so——"

"I didn't ask if you were hungry. I'm gonna fix you breakfast, you're gonna eat it, and if you don't like anything I said, then you can just talk about me behind my back," Imani stated, moving further away from our bedroom.

I couldn't suppress the chuckle that escaped my throat as I hit the blunt again and set it down in the ashtray. I stood up and headed into our walk-in closet, emerging ten minutes later looking more official than a government seal. Using my nose, I followed the heavenly smells of bacon and eggs to the kitchen, where I found Imani rapping along with Lil Baby as she cooked.

"I guess you can take a girl out of the hood, but..."

The look of annoyance she threw at me over her shoulder made me laugh as I took a seat on the bar stool at the center island in the kitchen.

"Stop acting like your Richmond-born ass ain't ratchet and willing to show it," Imani replied, turning back to the stove.

I almost decided to argue about Richmond, Virginia not being hood, but the truth was that most of it was. I'd grown up on the South side and had seen more shit than I cared to remember. My eyes were older than my 24 years on this earth, that was for damn sure, but all that I'd seen had made me better at my job.

"You got it, boo, I'm not even 'bout to argue with you," I said, putting my hands straight up as a sign of truce.

"That's smart, especially considering that I'm in the middle of fixing your food."

I chuckled, but kept my smartass comments to myself.

"What time is your meeting?" she asked, bringing my plate to me and setting it on the counter.

"In half an hour, at 9 a.m."

"You still don't have any idea what it's about?" she asked anxiously.

"Nah, but I'm not too worried about it. I know that I ain't done shit to be worried about."

The look we exchanged was an acknowledgement of the elephant in the room, which was my relationship with my father. Imani had been with me a long time, and she'd even been at my dad's coming home party when he finished his first prison bid. Still, she only knew the things I'd chosen to tell her, and that hadn't included the part where my dad executed my pregnant sister in front of me. She knew the things that were a matter of public record, like the fact that the cops thought he'd orchestrated a prison break so crazy that it was considered domestic terrorism. Luckily, Leroy and I didn't have the same last name, so I didn't have reporters lurking behind corners or camped out in front of my condo. Unfortunately, my bosses knew Leroy was my dad, and because of that, we'd had more than one conversation in the last two weeks about his possible whereabouts. I had no idea where the infamous Leroy Bly was, and I could only hope that wasn't the conversation topic at the meeting I was headed to with my department supervisors. I hated repeating myself.

"Well, no matter what they want, I need you to keep your hot-ass temper in check. You're a good cop, Lia, so just put the focus on that."

I nodded my head in understanding before beginning to eat my food. I got about five bites in before the meal was no longer attractive to me, and I pushed the plate away. Despite the frequency of my nightmares, I wasn't surprised at the timing today. My instincts told me that even if the meeting wasn't directly related to my father, it would still come up in conversation. Accepting this inevitability made me stand up and head back to my bedroom to finish getting ready. Once I stepped into the black dress shoes that went with my dark blue uniform, I put on my utility belt and grabbed my Glock .27 out of my gun safe. I found Imani in the kitchen cleaning up on my way out, and I paused to kiss her on the back of her neck.

"I'll call you later," I said, grabbing my keys and phone off the kitchen table.

"Be safe, bae," she called after me.

I made my way to my black-on-black GMC Denali, hopped in, and started the engine. Before pulling off, I sent a text to my partner asking him where he was at. Honcho and I had been partners since we'd graduated from the academy, but we'd known each other before then because he was from Richmond too. The first time he'd got arrested for some weed he'd called me, crying and begging me to get him out of Richmond city jail. I'd kept a straight face until he'd told me that he feared for his virginity because he was a pretty boy. I'd still been in tears laughing when I'd bailed him out two hours later, but he hadn't cared, and I'd been stuck with his ass ever since.

Once I texted him, I put my phone in the console and pulled off. It would only take me ten minutes to get to the police station in Henrico, which meant I didn't have to rush.

As badly as I wanted to smoke another blunt, I knew it wouldn't do me any favors to walk into a meeting with the brass smelling like bud. The only alternative was for me to hit the dispensary and grab some edibles, but I damn sure couldn't walk in there in my uniform. That shit would break the internet because somebody would DEFINITELY record it and post it. I waited until I came to a red light, grabbed my phone, and sent a text to my girl Brisha who worked at the dispensary I frequented. I let her know that I was on the way, and then I gave her my order for orange slices, gummy bears, a chocolate brownie, and a peanut butter cookie. By law, there was a limit on how much THC could be infused into edibles, but Brisha knew that I wouldn't tell that she had that overdose formula if she didn't. I was just one of many satisfied customers.

The sound of a car horn made me look up, anticipating the light having changed to green, but what I saw instead made my mouth go dry. A black panel van had boxed me in from the front, and a glance in my rearview mirror revealed an identical one behind me. Two men stood in front of my truck, and it was easy to see that the AR-15's they were holding were equipped with drums to hold the bullets they could unleash in seconds. I let my phone drop while raising my hands slowly and making sure not to make any sudden movements. Suddenly, a woman appeared at my driver side door and pulled it open.

"Nobody is gonna hurt you, Lia, I assure you. The guns are more for dramatic effect than anything else, but still, if I were you, I'd do what you're told."

"What the fuck do you want?" I asked with irritation dominating my tone.

"Get out of the truck and come with me. Your truck will be parked here, and you'll be returned to it later. Maybe."

I didn't move or speak for a second, I simply evaluated the woman who was politely trying to kidnap me. She couldn't have been more than 5'2", maybe weighing 150 pounds, which put us not far apart weight-wise while giving me at least five inches of height and a decent reach advantage. Whooping ass could get me shot though, so I needed a different approach.

"My momma told me to never go with strangers," I stated seriously.

"That's cute, Now get out," she replied, stepping back and motioning me forward.

I climbed down out of the truck with my hands still up, and I immediately saw her eyes go to my gun on my hip. As badly as I wanted to reach for it, I wasn't some dumb bitch who would panic. I took two steps forward, allowed her to remove my gun from its holster, and then followed her lead to the van in front of my truck.

"You can ride shotgun," she said, opening the passenger side door for me.

"Thanks," I replied dryly, quickly scanning with my vision to see how many traffic cameras were picking up on this bold heist.

Once I was settled in the seat beside the masked driver, the woman vanished, the two men holding the assault rifles climbed in the back of the van I was in, and we pulled off.

"Give me your hands," one man demanded from behind me.

I turned sideways in my seat and stuck my wrists out. Once the zip ties were secured on me, I turned back around so that I could watch where we were going. That mission was short-lived though because my world suddenly went dark when one of the men behind me threw a hood over my head. Instinctively, I struggled, but the grip he put on my neck to hold me steady spoke volumes about his workout regimen. So instead of doing the useless thing, I tried to meditate and center myself so that I could focus on how long we drove, and how many times we changed directions.

It was approximately an hour and fifteen minutes before we came to a complete stop, and I could hear doors opening around me. It took a few minutes for my door to be opened, and when it was, the hood was still not removed from my head. Someone grabbed me by the zip ties, helped me get my feet on the ground, and then led me away. I counted 47 steps before I came to a halt, and suddenly daylight was restored because the hood came off. I squinted and blinked rapidly to help my eyes to adjust, but even when they did, I still thought I was seeing shit.

"It's been a long time, lil one," he said.

"Obviously not long enough because you're still doing criminal shit, Leroy."

Chapter 3

Leroy

"Well, I wouldn't have been reduced to this method of communication, DAUGHTER, if you would talk to me like normal kids do with their parents."

"We ain't normal, and you're NOT my father," she said through clenched teeth and a piercing stare.

I knew she had a stubborn streak that was twice as strong as most kids because she'd gotten it from me and her mom, but I had to get through to her.

"Lia, listen, I didn't bring you out here for a family reunion or to talk about the mistakes of the past. I brought you here to try and make up for some of that."

"Somehow, I doubt that very seriously, but since you got me here, why don't you spit out whatever your reasons are so that I can go," she replied sarcastically.

"I know that everyone has been looking for me, thinking that I did some CRAZY shit, but I was nowhere near that prison."

"You're Leroy Bly, so since when do you have to be on the front line in order for your hired guns to carry out your demands? You can shoot the bullshit to someone else, because I know better," she said.

"Yeah, I figured that you would say some shit like that, which is why I'm willing to let my actions speak for me. I'm gonna turn myself in, and I wanted you to bring me in. So now you know why you're here."

My comment was met with an open-mouthed stare that was as comical as it was adorable, but she recovered swiftly.

"Leroy, you're full of shit. Why would you turn yourself in, and why would you involve me after all this time when you know that I don't fuck with you?"

"It's simple: because you're my daughter. I know that most of the world doesn't know that, but I'm sure your superiors in the Richmond police department do. That stands to reason that the feds know too, and I'm sure you've been questioned like your loyalty to your job was fake. I never wanted that for you, sweetheart, and I'm hoping that you bringing me in will smooth some things over for you," I replied.

My comments once again left her speechless, but I could still read the uncertainty swimming through her eyes. I motioned for Charlene to step forward from her position behind and to the left of Lia.

"Cut her zip ties off Charlene," I instructed.

Within seconds, Lia had full use of her hands and she rubbed her wrists to restore the blood's circulation.

"Give her gun back," I said, locking eyes with Lia over the top of Charlene's head.

Again, my commands were adhered to, and I saw the skepticism in Lia's eyes waver slightly.

"Do you wanna drive, or do you want me to?" I asked.

"You're really serious? Well, you're gonna have to drive, because this chick here made me leave my truck," Lia replied with irritation.

"I apologize for that, but we had to make it look good or there were sure to be more questions. People might think you knew where your dad was the whole time," Charlene said.

"Oh, those questions are still gonna come up, but I can see your point. I can't believe I'm about to ask this, but...Leroy, are you sure about this?" Lia asked.

This question caused Charlene to turn and look at me, because the exact same question had been asked by her more than once since I'd shown up on her doorstep.

"I'm sure," I replied, holding my own wrists out to be cuffed.

Lia paused for a second before holstering her gun and pulling the handcuffs out.

"I'll drive," Charlene said, nodding towards her silver Lincoln Navigator.

Once Lia had me cuffed, we followed Charlene, and we climbed into the backseat of the SUV.

"How do you wanna play it, L?" Charlene asked.

"Drop us off somewhere, and then she can call it in," I replied.

Charlene started the SUV and pulled off. I desperately wanted to talk to my daughter, to gain any bit of knowledge about her life in these last five years. Like any responsible parent, I'd kept tabs on her, but I gave her the space she needed. There was no way for me to know how Cyn's death had affected Lia, partly because I still didn't know how it affected ME, and I was the one who had killed her. I'd felt justified in that moment, but the aftermath was that I couldn't ever speak about it. Not even to Gini. I knew this wasn't a conversation that Lia and I were about to have, just like I knew that it had to be her to break the ice. We rode in complete silence until we were back inside Richmond city limits, and then Lia directed Charlene to a nearby Burger King. Once we got there, Lia and I got out of the SUV, and Charlene pulled off.

"What's next?" I asked.

She looked at me for a few seconds before looking up the street. I followed her gaze, and I could just make out a police station in the distance.

"That where we're going?" I asked.

"Yeah, but AFTER you tell me the truth."

"Lia, I told you——"

"I know what you told me, and I don't believe you. If you EVER want a relationship with me again, then you better tell me the truth now," she said.

I took a step closer to her and looked down into her upturned face so that she could look directly into my eyes.

"I did not destroy that prison," I stated calmly, yet firmly.

Her eyes scanned every inch of my face, undoubtedly looking for any of the signs that signaled deception. Once she was satisfied, she took a step back and motioned for me to walk in front of her in the direction of the police station. It took us ten minutes to reach the front door, and as soon as we walked through the frosted glass doors, all movement stopped like the record had been pulled on the music. Lia took control of the situation by grabbing my handcuffed wrists and pulling me into an interrogation room down the hall.

"Sit here, and don't say shit until I get back," she said, pushing me down into the uncomfortable plastic chair.

I didn't have a chance to respond before she was gone, and I was in an all too familiar position. I'd swore that I'd never be in anybody's jail or police station with cuffs on again, yet here I sat voluntarily, gambling with my life all in the name of love. In the back of my mind, I could hear my mom calling me a dumb ass. I blocked that out though and got comfortable, because I knew how the game was played. It didn't surprise me in the slightest when a full hour passed before the door to my windowless coffin was opened, and in stepped a short brown-skinned female. Her small, yet thick frame accompanied by the cute pink glasses she wore made her seem nonthreatening, but the oak leaf bars on her pristine white uniform told me better.

"I'm Commander Montgomery, Mr. Bly, and I'll be handling your questioning," she said, taking a seat across from me.

"Don't you mean interrogation, Commander?"

"If that's how you would prefer to label it, then that's you decision, Mr. Bly."

"I call a spade a spade," I replied, smirking.

"It was to my understanding that you surrendered yourself for questioning after thwarting a kidnapping attack on one of our police officers. Is that correct?"

"So are we really gonna act like the police officer ain't my daughter?" I asked sarcastically.

"It's to my understanding that Officer Panel doesn't identify as any familial relation to you, so we'll just refer to her in her official capacity. Now, do I have the facts straight so far?"

"Yeah," I replied dryly.

"Okay, good. Well, we do appreciate your bravery, and we'll discuss exactly how you were able to save Officer Panel later, but first things first. Let's talk about what happened two weeks ago."

"Can you be more specific?" I asked, feigning ignorance.

"Sure. I'm talking about when you orchestrated one of the deadliest attacks on U.S. soil just to get your wife, who was convicted of murder, out of doing her life sentence."

"That sounds like a great idea...for a movie, and some superheroes. I'm just a small business owner, Commander, not some evil genius plotting terrorist attacks," I replied sincerely.

"Okay, well let's back up about a week or so before that when your wife's codefendant's kids and mother were murdered by you."

I knew immediately that despite her nonchalant delivery, she'd intended to catch me off guard with this topic change, and she'd succeeded. I made sure not to give any outward indication of being startled, but I chose my words even more carefully. "I honestly have no idea what you're talking about, Commander Montgomery. Who was killed?" I asked.

"Are you suffering from selective amnesia, Mr. Bly? Because if so, then I'm sure I can have your homie Demon transferred from his holding cell over here, and then you two can get your story straight."

It was impossible to hide my shock this time, but all this did was put a smile on my face.

"Make sure you call my lawyer first," I said.

"Your lawyer? Is he or she a magician? Because if not, then they can't help you get your nuts out of this fire."

"Forgive me if I don't take your word on that, because I LOVE my odds of an acquittal with the brilliant legal minds at my disposal," I replied, smirking confidently.

"It's your life to gamble with, Mr. Bly, but if I was you, I'd consider the help that I can offer you before you get your legal team involved."

I didn't speak for a few seconds, allowing the suspense to build under the disguise of hesitation, hiding the truth of my calculation in the process.

"What type of help are you trying to offer?" I asked, measuring my words and tone carefully.

"If you help us put together the pieces of the puzzle for how you were able to successfully complete the prison break, then I can guarantee you immunity for the homicides involving your wife's codefendant's family. Along with that, you'll get a reduced prison sentence that would allow you to leave prison alive one day, provided that you give a list of your codefendants and their involvement. An ACCURATE list, please," she replied, pulling a pad and pen out of the desk in front of her before sliding it across the table to me.

I made no move to raise my cuffed wrists off the table. My fixed gaze stayed on the woman across from me as my mind ran in well-paced circles around the problems I needed to work through. The first thing I needed was more information, and suddenly the commander didn't seem like the source I required.

"That deal seems too good to be true, Ms. Montgomery. Whoever your boss is, they would NEVER sign off on any type of immunity deal for someone accused of mass murder,

UNLESS it involved a life sentence. While parole may have been reinstated in the state of Virginia, a life sentence for a capital crime is still 600 years. Mandatory minimum. For the deal you're offering to be real means it comes from somewhere above your pay grade, and for me to take it, I'm gonna need that person to be sitting where you are right now. You must always remember that the boss talks to the boss. Not the worker."

Chapter 4

Lia

"Okay, Officer Panel, let's go over your account of the incident again, starting with the kidnapping."

"With all due respect, Lieutenant Buttons, we've been going over the same territory for the past two hours. I'm exhausted, and as I'm sure you can understand, it's been a long day. Can we do this at another time?" I asked, rubbing my forehead in small circles to ease the tension.

I could feel the disapproval radiating from his 6'3", 280 pound hulking frame that was perched on the side of his desk a few feet from me, but he didn't press the issue. His response was to nod his bald head and stand up. I took that as my cue and quickly got to my own feet so that I could put some distance between the last three hours, which seemed surreal, and my actual life. Without a backwards glance, I strolled out of the windowless room with the stale air and headed up the hallway. It took me ten whole steps to realize that I was headed towards the room I'd stuck Leroy in, and I came to an abrupt halt. Most of the two hours had been about me vehemently denying working with my father, or knowing where he'd been hiding, so me going straight to him was bound to look crazy.

Luckily for me, there was a door leading to the stairway and out into the parking garage, so I didn't have to turn around, only adjust course. During my debriefing, Honcho had gone to retrieve my truck, and I was thankful for that now as I climbed up into the leather seat. Within seconds I was in motion, headed for home, where I could find some peace and quiet. I knew that I was gonna have to explain myself to Imani first though, so I began to formulate that story while driving.

When I pulled up to my spot, I was surprised to find that Imani's car wasn't there, but then again, I hadn't told her that I was coming home early. I chalked it up to more peace and quiet for me as I got out and headed inside. The first thing I did after locking myself into my safe space was strip off my uniform and head for the shower. I spent 20 minutes underneath the blistering spray of hot water, trying to really understand Leroy's motives, because that nigga didn't have a noble bone in his body. All he knew how to do was take, so him giving to anybody, even his own kid, made no sense. By the time I'd gotten out of the shower, threw on some comfortable clothes, and sparked a blunt, I still wasn't any closer to figuring out what angle the nigga was playing. That frustrated me! By the time I got to blunt number two, I didn't really give a fuck what Leroy had planned. I just knew that I didn't want no parts of it. I'd done my good deed for this lifetime, and I was out of whatever his play was.

I'd just put the still-smoldering roach in the ashtray when I heard someone come barreling through the front door. A quick glance told me that I didn't have to get up off the couch because it was just Imani.

"Hey babe, I'm in the living room," I called out.

I heard the door slam, and when I looked in that direction, I saw Imani moving like a train going downhill.

"I was just about to call you——"

"And tell me that you turned your dad in today?" she asked, stopping right in front of me.

"Huh?" I replied, dumbfounded.

"Too much weed clogging your brain? Let me help you out real quick," she said, pulling out her phone and sticking it in my face.

It took me a good fifteen seconds to focus so that the words on the screen would stop doing the Cha Cha Slide, and then I was able to read slowly. The headline on the news feed read that Leroy Bly was in the custody of the Richmond city police. It wasn't until I got three sentences into the first paragraph that what I read made my stomach drop.

"How the fuck does anyone know I'm his kid? Dead ass, the only people that know within the precinct are the supervisors and their bosses."

"And you think none of THEM will sell you out? Babe, that's not realistic," she said, pulling her phone away from my face and sitting down on the couch beside me.

My instant anger was directed at who it might've been that ran their dick sucking-ass lips, but I quickly rerouted that energy to further analyze what this meant.

"I mean, who gives a fuck who knows that me and Leroy share DNA? He and I are not the same."

"Baby, I know that, but your dad has enemies, and you're bound to inherit them now. After what happened to your sister, you don't realize that?"

I opened my mouth to object to her logic, but then I remembered the story the world had been told by me about who gunned down my sister in my home. It had been easy to sell the story of Leroy's enemies coming after him, especially since another shooting had taken place an hour prior to Leroy killing Cyn. Just thinking about how that son of a bitch had played the part of grieving father made me mad even now! I knew I had to let that go though, and focus on what to do next.

"I doubt that Leroy's enemies will take a run at a cop, babe, so don't trip off that shit. We're good," I said confidently.

"Lia, you know that I trust you with my life, I just think it's a great time to take a vacation."

"You think you got all the fucking sense too, when you know your ass is just trying to get me to dick you down on the beach," I said, laughing.

"Shut up! I'm just saying——"

Her statement was interrupted by the sound of wood splintering, followed by a deafening explosion. The couch flipped backwards like a tumbleweed in a western, tossing us along the way like a pair of plastic gloves in a tornado. My mind was instantly clear from the fog of the weed, and suddenly I was moving off of instinct.

"Imani, run!" I yelled, heading for our bedroom.

The sound of rapid gunfire reached my ears right before I hit the corner, causing me to flinch involuntarily in anticipation of catching a bullet. I didn't break stride though, bolting down the hallway at a dead run. When I got to my room, I didn't go for my pistol in my panty drawer. I headed for the closet to retrieve BIG MAMA. I could hear the bullets still ringing out loudly, approaching me as I snatched up my AR-15 and levelled it at shoulder height. I wanted Imani to be in the room before I let loose, but when a masked gunman popped into my sight, I let my finger caress the trigger. He danced for a few seconds and then dropped, but two more took his place. I never took my finger off the trigger until I heard what sounded like the balls from a pool table hit the floor right outside my bedroom door. I didn't have to look down because the sudden ceasefire and disappearance of my attackers confirmed my suspicions. Adrenaline took ahold of my body, and the next thing I knew, I was spinning around and lunging towards my bedroom window. My gun shattered the glass, and its weight carried me into a front flip out onto the grass. Seconds later, the world shook violently. Before I could get to my feet, the ground trembled again, and this time, the sound of screams could be heard. In my heart, I wanted to believe that those sounds of agony didn't belong to the woman I loved, but my gut was telling me something different. When I finally scrambled to my feet, I had every intention of going back inside for Imani, but I immediately saw that the threat had followed me outside. Two men were coming around the corner from the front of my building, which meant that they were blocking my path to my truck. A quick change of plan and direction had me running in the opposite direction, almost blinded by the tears streaming from my eyes. I knew that allowing any part of grief over whatever fate Imani faced to enter my mind would mean certain death, so I pushed it down inside me and ran faster.

My old high school days as a moderate track star came into play as I covered the distance of two blocks, zigzagging in between apartment buildings, in under a minute flat. I came out on a main street and stopped the first vehicle I saw headed in my direction. At first I was headed towards the driver's side with the intention to commandeer the truck, but then I saw who was driving and I froze. My first thought was to shoot straight through the windshield, and then I realized that she was motioning for me to get in. Time wasn't something I had, so I made the split-second decision and dashed for the passenger side door. I pulled it open and threw myself inside, but she already had us moving at a fast pace before I could shut the door.

"What the FUCK are you doing here, Charlene?" I asked, fighting to catch my breath while checking for more shooters out the window.

"What does it look like? I'm the fucking calvary," she replied, taking turns fast enough to have us up on two wheels.

For the moment I kept my mouth shut so that my suspicions wouldn't be telegraphed, and I focused on spotting a tail. After ten minutes of expert evasive driving I finally relaxed enough to lean my head back against the truck's headrest, and took my first deep breath since the shooting started.

"You're not here by coincidence, are you?" I asked, staring blankly at the ceiling.

"You're Leroy's daughter, so I know you don't believe in something as innocent as coincidence."

"You're right, I don't, which means I'm gonna need a clear answer as to how you just HAPPENED to be in the right place at the right time," I said, gripping the AR-15 resting in my lap, just in case.

"I'm here because your dad had us watching your spot from a distance just in case some shit happened. Leroy is paranoid to the point that it makes him clairvoyant sometimes, and there was no way he was gonna make himself so vulnerable that you would be too."

"I don't understand though, because Leroy is not vulnerable. He's in police custody," I reasoned.

"That's a joke, right?"

Her question made me look over at her, and there was some hot shit on my tongue for her insinuation about my brothers in blue.

"Oh my God, you're not joking," she said, staring at me closely.

"Why the fuck would that be a joke? ALL cops ain't corrupt, so you can miss me with that shit!"

"You're right, all cops ain't corrupt, but do you not know what your dad did five years ago?" she asked.

"He did a lot of fucked up shit five years ago, and no one knows that more than me."

"True...but I can tell that you don't know the whole story," she replied softly.

I let the silence hang between us for a few seconds that seemed like minutes, but then my curiosity won the battle of wills.

"What don't I know?" I asked.

"That your dad...he went on a killing spree..."

Chapter 5

Leroy

I didn't know if time was standing still or if the clock on the wall was broken, but it had been the longest 45 minutes EVER since Commander Montgomery had walked out of the room. I had no doubt that she'd return with some more bullshit, but my resolve was stronger than her determination. What I didn't understand was how they knew anything about me and Demon killing Pony's family, because I refused to believe that Demon had snitched on me. It was the plausible conclusion that the cops wanted me to jump to, but if they had me dead to rights, then I would've been fingerprinted and booked by now. Something wasn't right. I just didn't know what it was yet. The sound of the door opening shifted my attention to Montgomery and the slender-built brunette coming in behind her. I waited for Montgomery to speak, but she didn't.

"Mr. Bly, my name is Special Agent Eleanor Turn of the FBI, and I'm in charge of the Richmond field office. I was told by the commander that you wanted to speak with me regarding the deal that's currently on the table."

"Can I see your credentials, please?" I asked politely.

The smirk that popped up on her pretty white face was more arrogance than amusement, but she obliged my request by pulling her plain black wallet from her suit jacket and flashing her badge.

"Oh, a real live FBI agent in my presence. I guess this means that I finally made it," I said with feigned excitement.

"I'm glad this is all fun and games to you now, because it won't be in the end," Montgomery said, taking a threatening step towards me.

"Commander, would you mind giving us the room please," Turn said, watching me with the same intensity that I was watching her.

I could hear the heaviness in every breath that Montgomery took as she tried to calm herself until she left the room in obvious anger. The fact that she slammed the door on the way out made me smile and chuckle a little.

"This seems really personal to her," I said.

"You could say that. But I wanna focus on you, Leroy. I thought our offer was VERY generous, considering how many people you killed with your little prison break. Where did you find a problem?"

"You're right, the deal was, in fact, generous. It was TOO generous, which means that either I'm missing something, or I'm being lied to. I think I'm too smart to miss something at this point," I replied, leaning back in the chair.

"I will concede that you're intelligent, Leroy, but there's ALWAYS something that you're missing. Trust me. In this particular situation, though, it's pretty straightforward, so if you'll cooperate, then one day you'll know what freedom is."

Before I could ask another question, the door to the interview room was flung open, and in stepped a familiar face.

"Erin Gilse, Esquire, representing Mr. Bly. My client is done talking."

"Your client hasn't invoked his right to counsel," Turn stated.

"I just did," I replied.

The hate that filled Agent Turn's blue eyes made me tingle, and I realized instantly that I wanted to fuck it out of her in a good way.

"This deal is a limited time offer, Leroy, so I advise you not to let your mouthpiece fuck it up for you," Turn warned.

"Conversation OVER," Erin stated forcefully.

Before shit could heat up any further, Commander Montgomery reentered the room.

"We just received a shots fired call at your daughter's address, Mr. Bly. Do you know anything about that?" Montgomery asked.

"No, but is my daughter okay?" I asked, quickly standing up.

"That's unknown at this time. But your acting job of being a concerned parent needs some work," Montgomery replied before retreating the way she'd come.

The anger inside me built as swiftly as an unexpected summer storm, but I was able to keep my tongue still for the moment.

"Is my client being charged, or are you all just making empty threats in hopes that he'll build a case against himself?" Erin asked.

The silence from Special Agent Turn spoke loudly in the small room, but my mind was on Lia. I wanted to know if she was okay, and then I wanted the head of the nigga dumb enough to take a shot at one of mine.

"Get these goddamned cuffs off me," I growled through clenched teeth.

"Wait here," Turn said, walking out of the room.

"Well, Leroy, it looks like I got here just in time. What have I told you about talking to the cops without me? And a fucking FED at that?" Erin asked in frustration.

"You're sexier mad," I replied, smirking.

The fire in her hazel green eyes only got brighter, but that highlighted the blush she was trying to suppress. Erin Gilse was a top-notch lawyer, and the fact that she was drop dead gorgeous only enhanced how lethal an opponent she was. She stood 5'7" with a curvaceous 170 pound frame that made men and women stare, even before you saw the juicy ass she was equipped with. She kept her hair short, giving that innocent beauty of Demi Moore in the movie *Ghost*, and she was definitely capable of taking a nigga's soul. So far, she'd proven to be the best million dollars I'd ever spent.

"I just wanted to see what they had by way of evidence," I said seriously.

"That's what you pay ME for, Leroy."

"True, but sometimes women tell me things that they won't tell you," I replied, smiling mischievously.

"You're an arrogant, narcissistic motherfucker, Leroy, and it's gonna get your nuts clipped one day."

"And that's why it's up to you to keep that from happening. Besides, my nuts have values for you too," I said, widening my smile.

She laughed out loud and blushed hard enough to turn her sun-kissed skin red all the way up to her dark brown hair.

"Smartass punk. You're lucky I like you," she said, shaking her head.

Agent Turn came back in the room to find me smiling and my attorney laughing, and it was evident that these things took her from mad to hot fury within a few seconds. "Hold out your hands," Turn demanded angrily.

I did as instructed, and then I had full range of motion restored to my hands and wrists.

"Don't even THINK about leaving town, motherfucker, because you'll be back in cuffs faster than your pretty little attorney can orgasm," Turn said before turning to leave.

"I think she likes you," I said, winking at Erin.

"Oh, fuck you, Leroy!"

I laughed all the way to the front desk, where I waited to retrieve my personal affects. Once that was done, I followed Erin out to her cherry red AMG Mercedes coupe, already dialing Charlene's number on my phone. After two rings, the phone was answered.

"It's me and I'm out. What the fuck happened?" I asked immediately.

"I'll explain when I see you, but she's okay. I got her with me, and we're headed to safety," Charlene replied.

"What about Imani?" I asked.

"We'll talk about that later."

"Okay, I'm on my way," I said, hanging up and taking a deep breath.

"Everything okay?" Erin asked.

I could hear the genuine concern in her voice, which prevented me from giving any type of sarcastic response.

"Someone tried to kill my daughter."

"Oh shit," she replied immediately.

"The worst part is that my daughter is a cop, and I think it's her own kind that went after her."

"Wait, why would you think that?"

"Because they've always known she was my daughter, but she was useful because she was a way to get to me. So it's no coincidence that as soon as I'm in custody, someone targets her."

"I mean, I hear you, Leroy, but it really might be a coincidence."

"Did I forget to mention that I shot and killed a cop five years ago?" I asked in a deadpan voice.

"Yeah, you left that out. And it's no secret that cops have a LONG memory when it comes to shit like that. So, what are you gonna do?"

"I don't know. For now, I just need to get where my daughter is, so take me——"

"That's not your best move right now. I mean, you need to at least wait until the cops ain't watching you like a hawk so you don't lead them to her," she said.

I thought about her logic as I climbed into the passenger seat. She got in the car and got us moving, but she allowed the silence to hang in between us as I pondered my options.

"Where we going?" I asked after fifteen minutes of seemingly aimless driving.

"I'm taking you to my house, but I'm taking the scenic route so that we're not followed. My husband and kids are in upstate New York visiting family, which gives us seclusion to strategize your next move. The feds mean to nail your ass to the wall, Leroy, and you pay me a lot of money to keep that from happening. So just trust me a little."

I didn't reply verbally, but I nodded my head in consent to her plan of action. I sent a text to Charlene explaining the sudden change of plans, but I kept it vague as to where I'd be. I used the rest of the forty-minute ride to organize my thoughts and formulate the best moves to flush out my opponents. Once we pulled up to a picturesque split-level home tucked off into a gated community, my thoughts returned to the present problems.

"Are you expecting your family back anytime soon?" I asked, climbing out of the car and following her up the short driveway.

"Not for another few days at least. The kids needed some quality male bonding time, and plus...he and I needed some space."

I let her statement hang in the air as we entered her home because I didn't really know how to respond to it. I was the last person to give relationship advice, considering the amount of people I'd slaughtered for my wife. A love like ours wasn't simply rare. It was dangerous.

"I gotta make a call, but I don't wanna use my phone," I said.

"There's a landline in the kitchen. Just go straight down this hallway and make a right."

I nodded before following her directions. When I got to the phone, I quickly dialed the number to Gini's phone and waited. It only rang twice, and then I heard her voice come on the line.

"I'm good, bae, and I'm no longer in police custody," I said.

"That's great...but there's a lot you're not saying, so spit it the fuck out," she replied immediately.

Her sassiness made me smile, but I knew to still choose my words carefully.

"You know that nothing goes as planned, babe, but it's all gonna work out. Trust me. I need you to stay put and have faith in our plan."

"What plan, Leroy? You're out there hoping to eliminate the problem before it's verified. Do you even know where my sister wives are?" she asked.

"Sweetheart, I LITERALLY just got out of jail, and I haven't had time to do a damn thing except avoid arrest so far. Be patient and——"

"Fuck that patience shit! Do what the fuck you're there to do, or I'll come handle them bitches myself!" she yelled, hanging up on me.

"Love you too, baby," I said, shaking my head in frustration and hanging up the phone.

My eye quickly spotted the unopened bottle of VSOP cognac sitting on the kitchen counter, and I went straight to it. One twist of the top, and I had the whole bottle at my lips, gulping the potent amber-colored liquid.

"Take it easy, Leroy. I don't need you getting pissy drunk."

I lowered the bottle, intending to tell Erin some good advice about when it was appropriate to mind her own fucking business, but I pulled up short. The black leggings she'd changed into were gripping her curves like there was a seduction at work, and the oversized burgundy sweater hanging off her left shoulder only added to the sex appeal. I'd seen her in casual clothes before, but I'd never just taken time to appreciate her beauty.

"Wow," I mumbled.

"I'll take that as a complement...which is nice, because those are rare these days."

"If they are, then he's crazy," I said quickly.

Her blush was sudden, but even more adorable, and it made my stomach drop. She was trouble that I definitely wanted to get into.

Chapter 6

Lia

"Are you talking about the cop who tried to kill him?" I asked, choosing my words carefully.

"I think you know that the situation was WAY more complicated than that statement you just made, so how about we don't waste time bullshittin' each other? So, yes, I was referring to the cop and his crew that your dad killed in self-defense - the one your sister Cyn plotted with. It's deeper than that though."

I was just about to ask her what she meant by it being 'deeper', but our conversation was interrupted by her phone ringing. It was clear who she was talking to on the other end, but I was lost for a logical explanation as to how the fuck he'd gotten out so quick. I also wasn't entirely convinced that him being out was good for anyone. I didn't say anything though, I just listened to the brief exchange between him and Charlene while paying close attention to where we were going.

"You were saying?" I asked once she pulled the phone down from her ear.

"I don't know, what was I saying?"

"You were just about to explain why the cops are the real threat right now," I said.

"Well, the obvious answer is because your dad killed your sister's stepdad, the cop, but that's not where the story ends. Him killing Cyn...that shit destroyed something inside him that he's still unable to get back, but at least he's stopped lashing out from the pain. He still struggles with what he did, even if he'll never admit it, but it's nowhere near as bad as it was right after Cyn died. He lost his mind for 48 hours and went into a blind bloody rampage. He went after the dead lieutenant's partner, his boss, AND their families. It's bad enough when you kill a cop, but when you slaughter their family too..."

The weight of her statement merged with the silence that followed it, and I felt a chill creep up my spine. Listening to her, I could hear the truth in her words, but she wasn't speaking with any type of approval of Leroy's actions. I detected fear in her recounting, and that struck me.

"I-I don't remember hearing anything about these murders, and I was paying attention because of what happened at my house. I was paranoid about being next on Leroy's list of people who didn't need to breathe," I said, searching my memory for some hint of what she'd described.

"I suspect that you didn't hear about it because it was never a headline. Your dad is highly resourceful and intelligent, plus he has a lot of FRIENDS. Let's just say that slot of people came up missing."

"Well, if he's so good at doing his dirt in secret, then how do you know this?" I asked, eyeing her suspiciously.

"Because your dad and I don't have any secrets. We've come too far for that."

Her statement left me with more questions than it answered, but none of them seemed important when compared to figuring out how to stay alive.

"Okay, so you must think that the only reason my dad turned himself in was to protect me, but I'm not that naïve. His ass is up to something," I stated.

"Of course he is, but I don't ask. I just follow his lead."

"Just like that?" I asked curiously.

"Yeah, just like that."

When she glanced over at me, I only saw one thing swimming behind the cute rectangular frames of her glasses. I saw loyalty.

"The way that you say things sometimes tells me that you're not a part of the world that Leroy is bred from, yet you're completely loyal and devoted to him. Why?" I asked, turning in my seat to look closely at her.

"That's a long story, Lia."

"Obviously we've got time, and I need to talk about something to keep my mind away from the darkness," I said, feeling my heartache over thoughts of Imani trying to swallow my consciousness. Despite the years I'd spent perfecting my poker face, I knew that Charlene could see the still bleeding wounds of my soul when she looked over at me. She didn't pry though, and I was grateful for that.

"I met Leroy through his wife a while ago, while she was still in prison. I was a nurse back then, and I developed a soft spot for Gini because I honestly didn't think she deserved to be in prison for the rest of her life."

"Is this the same woman who had double life for robbery and murder?" I asked with disdain.

"Yeah, but it's not that simple. She actually didn't rob or kill anyone. It was all her boyfriend at the time, Pony. Pony was a junkie, and he got Gini hooked on drugs while abusing her in every way."

"Why the fuck did she stay with him?" I asked.

"If you've ever been in an abusive or toxic relationship, then you know it's not as easy or simple as walking out."

I had a dozen clichéd responses on the tip of my tongue, but I bit all of them back as a rogue thought about my own relationship crystalized in my mind. "I never met Gini, and I didn't know anything about her, so I'm gonna keep my mouth shut."

"Wise decision, Lia, but just know that Gini had love for you simply because you're Leroy's daughter. She knew about you, and she knew about Cyn. She NEVER wanted to take your place, or take your dad away from you. None of us did."

"So then why go along with his crazy-ass plans?" I asked with confusion and frustration.

"It's hard to explain because to be honest, I NEVER saw my life being what it is right now. I'm still happy though - happier than I can remember being in my old life. As for my choice to follow Leroy... All I can really say is that he's a force of nature that you can either get caught up in, or destroyed by. Sometimes it can be both, and that's the gamble we take. Why do I gamble? Because I've witnessed the beauty, even in the destruction, and I'd rather be a part of that than to live life without it. I know that probably doesn't make sense, but it's my truth."

I absorbed her words and allowed them to rattle around my brain. She was right. It didn't make ANY sense, but I knew the feeling of being caught up in the storms my father could create. It didn't feel like a choice all the time, it felt...inevitable.

"Once upon a time, I was in school to be a nurse, and I had a clear picture of what my life was gonna look like. And then my father murdered my sister right in front of me. It wasn't justice. It was revenge, pure and simple. That moment, that force of nature pushed me to change my plans, and I devoted my life to being a good cop. I devoted my life to justice, " I said reflectively.

"I get it, and I applaud you for being able to put your life back together after something so traumatic. I've been there."

"I doubt that," I replied sarcastically, looking out through the front windshield.

"I was there when Leroy executed my husband at point blank range. I was actually sucking Leroy's dick when he pulled the trigger, so it's more or less my fault," she whispered.

Her words caused my head to snap back in her direction. I didn't even need her to look me in the eyes because I could sense the truth in her words, and with that truth came the understanding of this woman's bond to my father. It was the definition of complex. We rode on in silence for another half an hour, finally pulling up at the same location I'd been brought to earlier.

"We're gonna be here until Leroy says otherwise. As much as I know you hate being told what to do, listening to us is the safest move right now," she said.

I wanted to bite my tongue off before admitting that I needed Leroy for any fucking thing, but it would be stupid of me not to recognize the danger I was in. As a cop, I knew how my brethren thought and felt about anyone who would dare harm another cop or their family. I wasn't simply vulnerable; I was expendable in the end, and the best shot I had at staying alive was to trust in the one man I swore I never would.

"I'll stay, but I want you to deliver a message to my father. You tell him that the moment I THINK he'll double cross me, I'll put him down like I would any other animal."

"You're definitely his child," she replied, chuckling as she got out of the truck.

I didn't crack a smile as I followed her. I wasn't sure if the temperature had changed, but I could feel a chill in my bones that felt like it would never leave. The slight breeze sounded like it was whispering Imani's name in my ear, and I could feel the tears I'd been warring against stinging my eyes.

"Where-where's your bathroom?" I asked as soon as I crossed the house's threshold.

"The room you'll occupy is in the back, straight down this hallway, and it has its own bathroom," she replied.

I wasted no time making a beeline in the direction she'd pointed, and I managed to make it to the toilet in time to release the projectile vomit from my throat. With each heave, I could taste my own tears mixing with the hot bile spewing from the depths of my stomach, and it only made me cry harder. I could feel the hysteria overcome my entire body, but I was helpless to push back against it. I threw up until there was nothing left for my body to offer up, and then I dragged myself into the shower. Fully clothed, I turned on the water and let it pound me. The tears didn't stop, and I didn't expect them to. Not ever.

Chapter 7

Leroy

"You want a shot?" I asked, extending the bottle towards her.

"Are you trying to get me drunk so that you can take advantage of me, Mr. Bly?"

"Erin, I would never——"

"Relax, Leroy, I'm only fucking with you," she said, taking the bottle from me and moving towards the kitchen cabinets. "Do you know how to play quarters?" she asked.

"Uh, yeah..."

"Do I detect fear in the tone of your voice? The great Leroy Bly?" she asked, smiling widely as she took a seat at the kitchen table while filling two shot glasses.

"No fear; just curiosity. You don't seem like the type to know about drinking games."

"Well, I got more than one education in college. So, do you want to play with me?" she asked with a hint of seduction in her voice.

"This seems like one of those GREAT really bad ideas...but fuck it, I'm in."

Her smile was instant and inviting, but there was mischief all in her eyes.

"Are you trying to get me drunk and take advantage of me?" I asked half-jokingly.

"I don't know, maybe. You trust me, right?"

The way she asked the question had me scrutinizing her face closely while I contemplated my answer. After all we'd been through and everything she had bailed me out of, it was impossible not to trust her.

"Yeah, I trust you, Erin."

"Good," she replied, reaching inside a cookie jar sitting on the table and pulling out a quarter.

"It's the jar we use for change in our pockets at the end of the day, and at the end of the month, the kids guess the amount. Whoever is closest to the amount decides how the money is spent," she explained.

"Aww, that's cute."

"Sarcasm will get you nowhere, Leroy," she said, bouncing the quarter off the wooden table with a quick flick of her delicate wrist.

Based on the arc alone I knew her shot was money, and the soft splash of liquor seconds later confirmed it. I chuckled ruefully, but I guzzled my shot without hesitation and didn't pull the quarter out of my mouth until the burning reached my stomach.

"Two can play this game, slim," I said, bouncing the quarter purposefully.

It clinked loudly against the rim, but it still found its intended destination with a satisfying splash. She smiled, tossed her shot back like a pro, and then stared me down with a determination that reignited the burning in my stomach. I knew it was on after that. Fifteen minutes later, I'd bucked six more shots, but I'd only managed to force three on her.

"I believe you downplayed just how good of an education you got in college, Ms. Gilse."

Her laughter proceeded the splash of her quarter finding its mark again, leaving me shaking my head while holding up the sign for a timeout.

"Poor baby, do you need a minute?" she asked teasingly.

"Fuck you, Erin!"

"I don't think you could in your current state of mind," she replied, laughing aloud.

I almost said some smartass shit, but I caught the gleam of challenge twinkling in her eyes and I held my words. Instead, I stood up and eliminated the inches that had separated us. When she looked up at me, I didn't see any uncertainty in her gaze, which prompted me to hold my hand out to her. She took it, pulling herself up so that her tantalizing lips were closer than objects in a car's side mirror. I hadn't desired another woman this intensely since I'd consummated my marriage to Gini in a spectacular fashion, but there was something about this woman before me. I slid my hands under her sweater and hooked my fingers into the elastic of her leggings before I began to ease them down over her hips. I pushed them down her thighs, and when they pooled at her feet, she quickly kicked her left leg free. Before I could stand back up, she put a hand on my shoulder, which made me look up at her. The way she nibbled her bottom lip was sexy enough to have my dick throbbing against my boxers, but I was focused on the hunger building in her eyes. My hands went to her hips, and I lifted her effortlessly onto the table behind her. I slid onto the seat she'd vacated, using my left hand to press on her stomach to make her lean back, while my right hand put her left leg on my right shoulder. She opened for me without hesitation, and she smelled every bit as intoxicating as I'd imagined. I'd never started with this part of the sexual experience with a virtual stranger, but I quickly threw caution to the wind and took a long, lazy taste of her sweetest sugar. As soon as my tongue reached her clit, I could feel her heartbeat, and it was stronger than tectonic plates rubbing together. When my lips locked onto her delicate nub, I heard her breath freeze in her lungs, and her leg suddenly hooked behind my head, pulling me deeper into her blissful darkness. My mouth moved with the slow diligence of a seductive kiss, until my tongue shot out at her clit like a snake striking its prey. When her other leg wrapped around my neck, I knew she was running towards the end of the earth. The seduction of my mouth had her harmonizing my name as the pressure within her built, and it was music to my ears. I could feel her body trembling all around me as her thighs gripped my head tighter, and I knew she was almost there. Flattening my tongue against her clit, covering it with the rough texture of my taste buds, and applying just the right amount of speed to the pressure, killed her.

"Ohhhh-my-GOD!" she moaned, gasping for air while her orgasm pinned her to the hard wood table in Christ-like fashion.

All the deliciousness of her pussy juices filled my throat, banishing the taste of liquor from my memory. I drank from her like drowning was never an option. I waited until her convulsions had been reduced to tremors before standing up, and pulling her to the end of the table. In a split second, my dick was in my hand, and I was guiding it in between the heat of her pussy lips.

"You want it?" I asked, starring into her cum-dazed eyes.

"Can you h-handle it?" she countered, smiling lazily.

I accepted her challenge by pushing my dick all the way inside her with one slow, deliberate stroke. Once I was inside her, I paused to let the ringing in my ears subside, but after a few seconds, I realized it was not my warning of fulfillment. It was my phone going off. I had every intention of ignoring it, until I recognized the ringtone, and then I was digging in my pockets frantically.

"You're n-not really gonna answer," Erin said, reaching for me.

"Shhh," I replied, pulling my dick halfway out and pushing back inside her swiftly. "Hey baby," I said, fighting for control of my voice.

"Where are you?" Gini asked impatiently.

"Consulting with my lawyer at the moment. Can I call you back?"

"No, I need you to pause on that because you've got business to handle. We've located Amelia and Candice," Gini said.

Hearing this made me pull my dick completely out of Erin and take a step back.

"Fuck!" Erin whined.

I gave her a death stare to silence her while shaking my head vigorously. "Okay, send me the location," I said, hanging up before she could ask me anything.

"Can we finish now?" Erin asked with a sexy pout.

"I would love to, but I've gotta tie up these loose ends before I have to give you another million dollars of my hard-earned money."

Understanding flooded her eyes, causing her to sit up and hop down off the table. Instead of getting dressed, she bent down and pulled her other leg free of her garments, and then reached out to grab my dick. When she looked up into my eyes, I could still see her sexual fires burning, and I ached to blaze within them like one of the devil's spawn.

"This should help you to remember what's waiting for you," she said softly, while rubbing my still hard dick with her cotton panties. After she had succeeded in absorbing her pussy juices and cum into the fabric, she stuck the panties in my pocket and tucked my dick back into my pants.

"You're something else," I said, chuckling as I pulled her to her feet.

I kissed her lips softly, yet possessively, in an attempt to burn my own desire onto her soul like a fresh brand. When I pulled back, I looked down into her still-closed eyes, and smiled at the obvious disturbance I'd caused inside her usually stable spirit.

"I need a ride," I said.

Her eyes fluttered open slowly, and her smile spread with the beauty of a summer sunrise. "Take whatever you want, baby, including me."

"Oh, I will, just as soon as we can enjoy all that our chemistry has to offer. Right now though I need something fast moving, yet inconspicuous," I replied.

"Take my husband's Suzuki GSX-R 1300. It's in the garage, and the key stays in the ignition."

"I'll be back as soon as I can," I promised, dropping a quick kiss on her lips before moving past her.

I found the midnight-blue bike in the garage easy enough, and I admired her man's tastes once more as I climbed on the powerful beast. Thankfully, the helmet fit once I put my locks into a ponytail, and as soon as I fired up the engine, the garage door came up. I checked my phone to find my destination, sent two quick text messages before putting the phone back in my pocket, and then I took off.

From past experience, I knew that the drive from Richmond to Northern Virginia would take an hour and a half if all traffic laws were obeyed. I made it to the Denny's restaurant in Alexandria in 40 minutes flat, which was a personal best record at reaching 150 MPH moving through traffic. I didn't go inside the restaurant, choosing instead to post up in the corner of the parking lot and wait. A short 20 minutes later, as the night was starting to firmly close in around me, I felt the ground rumbling before the sounds of engines found my eardrums. I counted 10 Nation of Rulers, headed by none other than my man Zuk, who was one of the co-founders of this exclusive bike club. Zuk was the only one to climb off his bike and come over to me, but I could sense the readiness in all our soldiers.

"What's up, L? I wasn't expecting to see you this soon, and definitely not back in Virginia."

"There was no way to outrun this particular betrayal, so I had to face it head on. You know that I'm the type to get my hands dirty, especially when its personal," I stated emotionlessly.

"Yeah, I know. So, where we headed, and what's the plan?"

"My wives are being protected by the feds at a hotel in Maryland, so that's where we're going," I replied.

"Okay. Are we just gonna run in with guns blazing?" he asked, sounding skeptical.

"Nah, bruh, I've got a couple ideas that I'll explain once we get there. Trust me, it'll be fun."

Chapter 8

Lia

I lost track of time, curled up in the fetal position on the shower floor, but I managed to come back out of my catatonic state when I felt someone's hands on me. In truth, I was too emotionally distraught to fight back, and the ache in my soul had me believing that death would bring me more comfort right now. When I saw Charlene's face come into view, I didn't feel relief or anger. I only had room within me to feel despair. It took me a while to realize what Charlene was doing after she had my soaking wet clothes off of me, but I didn't fight her. I let her bathe me like I'd longed for my mother to do since she'd passed away, and I cried more silent tears of mourning. When she was done, she led me from the shower into the bedroom and she sat me down on the bed. It was a struggle to keep my puffy, burning eyes open, but something told me that even if I laid down, I still wouldn't find sleep.

"Wait right here," Charlene said, walking out of the room and heading up the hallway.

I didn't know that I wanted to be here, accepting help from my father by proxy, but I honestly had no idea where in the world I'd go. I'd already been estranged from any family I had left, but I hadn't cared because I had Imani at the end of every day. Now she was gone, and I had nothing left to save me from drowning. That meant one of two things: either I accepted the death that was certainly waiting on me, or I accepted my father's port in this storm of life.

"Here, smoke this, and put this on," she said, handing me a blunt the same size as a hotdog while tossing a black sweat suit on the bed beside me.

I smoked the blunt in silence until I felt the pressure lift a little from my chest, and then I passed it to Charlene.

"Thanks," I said softly.

"It's no need to thank me."

I was grateful for the fact that Charlene didn't feel the need to fill the silence with meaningless clichés about losing someone you love. We sat there and polished off the blunt, and then she left me alone to enjoy my solitude. I knew from past experiences that grief didn't have a timeframe on it, but I also knew when I'd let enough out to be able to push forward. After sitting around for a while I got up, pulled the clothes on that she'd left, and then I went in search of human life. As soon as I stepped out of the room, the smell of pasta sauce being cooked punched me in the nose hard enough to make my stomach burp. I found my way to the kitchen, where I discovered Charlene moving around with ease and obvious expertise.

"I know I'm high, but DAMN, it smells good in here," I said, pulling up a stool to the center island in the kitchen.

"Thanks. It's my grandma's recipe for homemade spaghetti. It always used to make me feel better when I was little, and now it makes me feel good to be able to cook it."

"You could open a restaurant based on the smell alone," I said, licking my lips just so they could absorb some of my mouth's moistness.

"That's sweet of you to say, but my family is from the old country, and they didn't believe in sharing recipes with anyone who wasn't la familia."

"Makes sense, I guess. Are we here alone?" I asked, looking around the spacious kitchen, and out into the dimly-lit courtyard through the glass doorway.

"Inside the house, yes, but the perimeter is surrounded by men loyal to your father. We've got plenty of firepower in here too, which I'll show you after you finish eating."

"You said men loyal to my father? What does that mean? My father has hired guns like that?" I asked, confused.

"How much do you wanna know, Lia?"

"I want to know what I NEED to know," I replied, locking eyes with her.

She nodded her head, adjusted some knobs on the stove, and then took a seat across from me. "In your official capacity, have you ever heard of a biker club called The Nation of Rulers?" she asked.

"Of course I have They've got chapters all across the country and into Canada. They've got a reputation for making some serious money, which doesn't come without equal serious violence."

I waited for her to say something else since she'd just been nodding while I was speaking, but no words left her mouth.

"Are you-are you saying that my father is a part of the Nation of Rulers?" I asked, feeling dumb for not putting the pieces together sooner.

"Well, sort of, I guess you could say that."

"Now ain't the time for evasive shit, so just tell me what it is," I said with mounting frustration.

"He's a leader inside the Nation of Rulers, number three in charge, to be exact."

"Ohhhh," I murmured, finally grasping why every law enforcement task force with a letter in its name would think he was capable of pulling off the massive prison break in the name of freeing his wife. "He lied to me. He looked me right in my motherfucking face and lied to me," I said, tasting the rage forming around the ugly truth.

"I don't know what you mean, but if he did, then I can assure you that he had his reasons, sweetheart."

"Yeah, he did. He's incapable of doing anything else or being anyone other than the twisted, murdering son of a bitch that he is," I said bitterly.

She wisely didn't try to defend him to me, but instead chose that moment to get up and return to the stove. Not even the delicious smells of the food combining with the fresh garlic bread she was pulling from the oven could distract me from the ugly truth right now. My father, the supposed reputable businessman, was in fact nothing more than a gangsta on a motorcycle. I didn't know if I was angry because of who he really was, or if it was just because of how stupid I felt for believing him to be something different. Right now, all I knew for certain was that I was PISSED!

"Did my dad destroy that prison?" I asked, staring intensely at the back of Charlene's head of black curls.

"That's a discussion for you and him to have."

"He's not here, so I'm asking you. Did he blow up that prison to get his wife out?" I asked again, battling to control the building fury within me.

Charlene suddenly stop working with the food, and turned around to face me. "You strike me as a wise young woman, Lia, which means that you know better than to ask questions that you don't want answers to. If you don't approve of your father's duplicitous lifestyle, his tactics, or his decisions, then I suggest you don't ask the types of questions that you're asking. You'll only succeed in disappointing your damn self."

Before I could say anything, she turned back around to the food and went back to work. I wanted to talk crazy to her muthafuckin ass, but we both knew that my issue was with my sperm donor and not the woman making me comfort food. This realization didn't dampen my anger, but it allowed me to suppress it for a later date. After taking a few steadying, deep breaths, I made room in my mind for the new information I'd just received to be analyzed more in depth. My mind went back to the day Cyn died, but instead of feeling that paralyzing numbness that had held me in a vise grip that day, I looked at it for signs of this new truth. I hadn't known the man that my father had called for help, but as I closed my eyes now, I could see him outfitted in the red, white, and black vest that I later came to recognize as the Nation of Rulers colors. The man who had shown up at my house had been a 1%er, and he'd come as soon as Leroy called. Because of what had happened that day, I'd vowed to never be involved with my father, but learning that he was a Ruler meant that I'd been chasing his trail of crime almost every day of my career. The world wasn't just small; it was cruel with sarcastic humor.

Charlene interrupted my train of thought by sitting a big plate of food in front of me while mumbling something in Italian. As badly as my pride wanted to slide the plate off the table and onto the floor, my stomach knew that a bitch this hungry wasn't gonna do nothing crazy. I picked up my fork and began eating, but my mind was nowhere near being distracted from its hamster wheel of thought. Even as I was burning my tongue while shoveling the hot food into my mouth, I was already watching a plan take form within my consciousness. I wanted the truth, and since it was obvious that both Charlene and my father thought I couldn't handle it, I was gonna have to find another source. I waited patiently for Charlene to join me at the table before I spoke again.

"Do you trust everything that Leroy tells you?" I asked.

"I trust that he'll tell me the things that I need to know to keep me safe. The more information one has, the more of a liability they become, and since I never want to be that, I don't ask a lot of questions."

"Okay, but you're obviously not naïve as to who Leroy is, and you're just good with that?" I asked.

"It wouldn't make any difference if I wasn't good with it, because he is who he is. From my perspective, I see him as more good than bad, and that's personally refreshing. You may need him to be more, but like I told you before, I caution you not to set unrealistic expectations, because you'll only break your own heart in the end."

I knew that she was telling the truth simply because I'd been breaking my own heart with expectations of my daddy since I'd been a little girl trying to discover his true identity. I'd imagined him to be like all the men I saw on TV and in movies who took care of their families and helped raise their children. By the time I was ten years old, my imagined daddy hadn't shown his face, and the man my mother chose to play his position had done things to me inspired by the devil himself. When I lost my innocence, I'd lost my hope in having a real dad, which had ultimately led to this exact moment in time. I wouldn't lie to myself about who Leroy Bly really was, but I had every intention on using him to stay alive. It was the least he could do for me.

"Charlene, I don't want any more lies, and I'm not building any illusions in my mind about my father. I simply want to know who he is for real. I can respect if you don't wanna tell me...but then I need to ask you for a favor."

"What's that?" she asked skeptically.

"For him to go through all the trouble that he is for one woman to be by his side, then she must know him better than anyone. So, I think it's time for me to meet Gini, and then, just maybe, she can introduce me to the real Leroy."

"How would you meet her if she's dead?" Charlene asked, eating her food slowly while staring at me.

"Because we both know that she ain't dead. Now, are you gonna help me or not?"

Chapter 9

Leroy

"Damn, the feds got it in their budget to rent out the top floor of the Hilton now?" Zuk asked, passing me the binoculars he'd been looking through.

"You know rats live in style in this day and time because snitching is as celebrated as shooting niggas in their faces used to be," I replied, shaking my head in disgust.

"I can't argue with that, even though it's all the way fucked up. What's your plan for getting in there though, L? You can see that they've got the ground and the roof covered."

He hadn't lied when he'd said that the feds were on high alert because so far, we'd counted two different eight-man teams: one on the roof, while the other was holding down the perimeter. The people on the ground were doing their best to blend in with the patrons coming and going, which was why they were dressed more like they were headed to the MGM casino. They weren't too obvious, but even from the vantage point of the hotel room window I was standing in right now two blocks away, I could pick a fed out in the dead of night. The question was, could I hit them from where I stood? The people on the roof wore tactical gear, and they weren't trying to blend in with anything other than the darkness surrounding. Despite the long way between the ground and the roof I knew that the feds on the roof were the immediate threat, which made them my primary targets.

"What's the count on Rulers?" I asked.

"Counting the ones we picked up on the way, we're at 26 right now, but more can come if you think it's necessary."

That amount would cover the outside, but who knew how many agents or cops were actually inside the hotel? As crazy as it sounded, I needed this hit to look only semi-professional, but I still needed it to be pulled off flawlessly.

"Okay, here's the plan I'm thinking about. You and I are gonna clean the rooftop while ten Rulers can go inside the hotel and set it on fire. Ten more Rulers can be outside to eliminate those threats as soon as possible. Easy as 1,2,3," I said confidently.

"Easy, huh? Well, we can make it more interesting if you'd like, L. So, let's do it old school like a video game, and we'll make each person you or I shoot worth 100k in cash. Whoever has the most kills collects at the end. Agreed?"

"I like where you're going with this, but we've gotta up the ante on my wives because they'll be moving targets, heavily guarded. Let's make it 250k apiece for them," I reasoned.

"Fair enough, but don't feel bad when I win. I own the high score for all shooting games played in my house, and believe me, my kids HATE that shit."

"Whatever, you ole Call of Duty-ass nigga. Just make the call, grab your weapon, and meet me on the roof," I replied, chuckling.

While he pulled out his phone to deliver instructions, I walked over to stand in front of the king-sized bed full of weapons. It had been fortuitous that the feds had made the decision to hold up at a hotel on the casino strip because I knew a lot of people who owed me favors.

Us being able to stroll right into the Double Tree hotel two blocks down, with all types of weaponry, was one of those favors in motion. All cameras being disabled was another important favor I'd had to call in because I'd needed that done for the hotel and the strip. The last thing I needed was all cameras swinging in one direction once the shooting started. My initial plan had been to use a bomb made of Semtex in hopes of levelling a city block, but that could make mass explosions my signature move in the eyes of the law. Later on, that could make me predictable. It would also strengthen the criminal case they were trying to build against me, plus bring more feds. Still, I was prepared for emergencies should I need to change strategies on the fly.

I opened two different cases and inspected their contents until I was satisfied that I had exactly what was necessary. I closed them and then got Zuk's attention to let him know that I was headed for the roof. When I got into the hallway, I passed one of the cases to a Nation of Rulers prospect, and he fell into step behind me as I headed for the stairway. Once I got to the roof, it took me about five minutes to assemble the stolen military sniper rifle that I'd carried up. By the time Zuk joined me I had the weapon properly calibrated and resting comfortably on its tripod in the southeast corner of the rooftop.

"We're all good on the ground. Just tell me when to go," Zuk said, opening up his own rifle case and putting his gun together.

While he did that, I got comfortable on the ground so that I could look at the activity a couple blocks away. The feds on the roof looked very disinterested in their assignment, based on the exasperated expressions on their faces. I had no doubts that once the shooting started that their instincts would come alive, but it would already be too late. The ground activity was a little livelier, but undoubtedly that was because standing still would look TOO obvious.

"You ready?" Zuk asked, laying down beside me.

"I'm always ready, bruh. Tell our men not to go inside though, and just focus on keeping more feds from sneaking in behind them. You and I can handle the building. I mean, if you've still got it."

His response was a chuckle that floated up and off the side of the building as he retrieved his phone. The call was made, and the order delivered.

"You remember what Candice and Amelia look like?" I asked

"I remember."

"On my mark then," I said, peering through the scope once more.

The first face I locked in on was covered by a black baklava mask, but it was easy to tell that he was a white guy in his 20's or early 30's. The displeasure of his current assignment was evident by his body language, which made me feel a little better about putting him out of his misery. After taking a slow, steadying breath, I squeezed the trigger slowly. In less than a second, the high velocity Teflon .223 round knocked a chunk of the agent's head off that included his left eye and a portion of his nose. Before his body crumbled to the ground, I'd adjusted my sights to lock in on the man five inches to his left, and quickly double tapped the trigger. The two head shots caused his brain matter to suddenly appear like when Lebron James tosses powder in the air before a game. I heard the sweet sigh of Zuk's rifle beside me come to life right before another agent met his untimely demise.

"Game on," I said, picking out my next target from those scrambling for cover.

A muscular-built black dude sprinted for the door that would've led to the stairway and back to safety, but my first shot blew his right kneecap cleanly off. I expected him to collapse on the spot, and I was anticipating the angle of my kill shot, but when he hit the ground, his eyes were already glassy with death from the hole in his head.

"Your assist, my kill," Zuk said.

"Sneaky muthafucka," I mumbled, moving on to the next person.

Switching my focus to the street, I could tell that the feds knew they were under attack. I spotted a man and a woman posing as a cute young couple until standard issue Glock .40's appeared in their hands, and the look in their eyes morphed into one of lit steel. They were scanning any and all faces within their immediate vicinity, which turned out to be their fatal mistake. I dropped them both like ice cubes into a glass of white Hennessey liquor. Naturally, the sight of two dead people caused immediate hysteria amongst the people who were just out to enjoy their evening. At first people stared, but then they took off running in every direction.

"Keep your eyes open. They know we're here," I said, already swinging my rifle in search of a new target.

Movement on the roof in the distance caught my eye, but I was only in time to see Zuk knock two dudes off the building with well-placed chest shots center mass. My eyes went back to the street, where I saw the other FBI agents converge in front of the hotel entrance.

"This is too easy," I said, half-chuckling as I let more shots ring out through the night.

"That looks like Amelia headed towards the south stairway or elevator," Zuk said.

I could feel the sudden eagerness explode within my chest as I shifted my attention to my soon-to-be ex-wife. Through the floor to ceiling hallway window, I could make out Amelia surrounded by feds, and they were moving with the precision of the President's private detail. Seeing her put a genuine smile on my face, and I could feel the electricity race to my fingertips in anticipation. The window of opportunity was closing fast because from the looks of things, she was headed for the elevator.

"Do you see Candice?" I asked, looking past Amy for more movement.

"Nope," Zuk replied, squeezing off two shots in quick succession.

The window in front of Amy shattered and another agent dropped, but he'd missed her by a centimeter.

"Close, but no cigar," I said, rolling away from my rifle and grabbing the other case I'd brought with me. It took me less than a minute to put the mini rocket launcher together, but picking my target took a little longer.

"All dressed up and nowhere to go?" Zuk asked, chuckling as he let off more shots.

"Funny, nigga, but make sure you pay me my money when it's over."

Before he could reply, I'd completed my estimation of where the elevator carrying Amy should've been in its descent to the underground garage. With a tap of my finger, the night came alive with a loud screeching sound. Seconds later, the hotel on the opposite end of my sights shook violently as one whole floor was instantly deleted from the blueprints forever. There was an eerie silence following the explosion, and then the agony of screams filled the smoke-filled air like pollen during allergy season.

"Yo, L, that's cheating and you know it bruh!" Zuk said, standing up and beginning to break down his weapon.

"I didn't know there were rules about weapon choices. You did have the same options as me, but you didn't think big enough."

"There's a difference between big and COLOSSAL," Zuk said, pointing at the now-flaming building in the distance.

The sounds of sirens ruled our debate over and shifted my attention to packing everything up as fast as possible.

"Time to go. I want everybody in the wind within ten minutes," I demanded.

Zuk nodded while pulling his phone out. I did a quick cleanup of our spent shells, putting them in the case with my rifle, and then I followed Zuk back down to our hotel room. We arrived to find members of The Nation of Rulers loading up the remaining weapons so that they could be taken downstairs to different waiting vehicles. It took us about five minutes to leave as quietly as we'd come, but it wasn't a moment too soon because I could feel the pressure of the feds tingling the hairs on the back of my neck. There were some red and blue lights in my side mirror, but not enough to convey the powerful presence of the octopus known as government law enforcement. I knew they were there though.

We all went in different directions so as not to appear so obvious as a motorcycle gang travelling together, despite helmets hiding our individual identities. I had no doubt that I'd be suspect number 1-10 when it came down to the "who done it" questions, but I wasn't worried. My mind was already looking ahead to solidifying my alibi, and as soon as I got a mile away from the scene of my latest crime, I opened up the throttle on the bike. The rush of feeling the raw power of the crotch rocket as it galloped at 192 mph was only rivalled by the shooting clinic I had just participated in on the roof. It was beyond an adrenaline rush to drive this fast or shoot people at will. It was godlike, and that type of intoxication was deadlier and more addicting than heroin laced with fentanyl. Within 25 minutes, I was easing the borrowed bike of my dreams back into my lawyer's garage, and I found her waiting for me by the door that led into her house.

"You didn't have to wait up for me," I said.

"Yes, I did, because if this is your work on the news, then you're soooo gonna need an airtight alibi."

Chapter 10

Lia

"I hear what you're saying, Lia, and I wanna help you, but as far as I know, Gini is dead."

"Bullshit!" I replied with mounting frustration.

"I swear to you on everything that I love that I haven't seen Gini since the day the prison was attacked, and for obvious reasons, I haven't spoken to your father about her. You think Leroy is just some monster without a beating heart, but he loves and he feels more than you know. He's grieving right now."

"Whatever. He doesn't know how to grieve, and if you think he does, then you're fucking brainwashed, or dick-matized. Either way, you're stupid," I replied, standing up abruptly and leaving her to finish the meal alone.

I understood that I hadn't spent any real time around my father so I wasn't an exact expert on him per se, but I'd grown up around fuck niggas. The one universal truth about my father, and all fuck niggas worldwide, was that they didn't change their spots. The most they did was get dirty so that the spots were camouflaged, thereby tricking most people looking at them. I wasn't gonna let Leroy trick me, but it was obvious that the people he'd surrounded himself with wouldn't be my allies. I was gonna have to trust my own people, and because of what happened to Imani, the list of people I could trust was almost nonexistent. From where I was sitting, my only two options were either my girl Brisha, or my partner Honcho. As painful as it was for me to admit it, I knew I couldn't trust the blue wall of law enforcement to protect me right now. Their hatred for my father overrode whatever love they'd had for me, if the love was ever real to begin with. I couldn't focus on those questions right now though because right now was about surviving, and to do that, I needed information.

Brisha worked in the weed dispensary by day, but at night, she morphed into Glitter, one of the most elite strippers in Virginia. She knew a little bit of everybody, and that was about to come in handy. I hadn't remembered seeing any phones throughout the house, but I began searching the bedroom I'd been given, looking for a landline. It wasn't until this search that I noticed the cell phone and pistol that had been left for me on the nightstand by the bed. Seeing these things almost made me feel bad for going hard on Charlene, but I didn't have time for all that soft shit.

I dialed Brisha's number from memory, and while it rang, I closely inspected the HK 9mm automatic pistol. At first glance, the 30-round clip seemed excessive for a small pistol, but then I recognized just how fast this bitch would spit because it was fully automatic. It would damn sure be hard for me to miss a muthafucka. When Brisha didn't answer, I sent her a text message so that she'd know it was me calling from a new number, and then I used the Wi-Fi to check the news reports. It wasn't a conscious effort to look for information about want had gone down in my neighborhood, but before I knew it, I was looking at images of my gutted condo decorated with crime scene tape. The article attached to the pictures said the body of an unidentifiable woman had been found, and the way it was worded implied that it was me dead instead of Imani. I had a hard time believing that someone did that on accident, which meant there was a person or persons who wanted the world to think I was dead already. The question I had was, was that done to protect me, or simply kill me any time without having to explain?

The more I thought about it, the more paranoid I got, and suddenly I was convinced that the evil I knew in the form of Leroy Bly was better than the evil I couldn't see. After reading the article for the third time, I lost the fight with my tears again, and silent streams poured from my eyes for the love of my life that was taken from me. I hated crying, but I was helpless to stop it, so I just let it happen. Once I was able to pull myself together, I looked down at the phone in my hand with the intention of moving on to something else, but a different surprise had popped out instead. A breaking news bulletin was flashing across the screen, and clicking on it brought me the latest info about an active shooter situation at the MGM casino in Maryland.

The world was so crazy these days that mass shootings were becoming normalized, but what stuck out to me about this shooting was that the FBI appeared to be the intended target. There were a few civilian casualties, but there were twelve feds killed and more hanging on to their lives in the ICU. I didn't know too many people bold enough to take a shot at the feds. Actually, I only knew ONE lunatic crazy enough to cause the destruction I was seeing. The question was, why? I read everything I could about the situation, but the news was careful to say a lot without saying a damn thing. It was obvious to me that they had a very good idea of who was responsible for this unnecessary loss of life, but I wanted to be as sure as they were.

Hopping up off the bed, I made my way back into the kitchen, where I found Charlene putting away the last of the leftovers from our late dinner.

"Where's my dad?" I asked, pulling up beside her.

"I don't know at the moment, but probably taking care of business to clear his name."

"Oh, is that what you would call this?" I asked, handing her my phone.

She took it, looking at me skeptically before resting her eyes on the screen. I watched her as she read, and it was fascinating to see her body literally protect itself by going numb. If I hadn't been standing in front of her to witness the transformation with my own eyes, I wouldn't have known what it looks like when someone becomes indifferent to something horrible. By the time she passed me the phone back, her eyes were void of any emotion, but I understood now how she'd been able to stand beside my father this whole time. She just turned herself off to the madness.

"What makes you think he had anything to do with this?" she asked.

"Is that a serious question right now? We both know that he's capable of this and so much more, but I understand if you don't wanna admit it."

"It's not about admitting or denying. I'm just asking why think your father was involved?" she asked calmly.

"My intuition tells me that its him."

"Oh...well, I don't know what to say about your intuition," she replied, going back to putting the food away.

I didn't know whether to scream first or punch her in the damn face, but both options were very tempting. Unfortunately, neither approach would accomplish much, so doing something different was the play.

"Call him for me," I said, holding the phone back out to her.

"For what?"

"I didn't know that I needed a reason to speak with my own father," I replied sarcastically.

She stood there and looked at me for a second, but then she took the phone and dialed a number. By the time it started ringing, it was fair to say that we were both holding our breaths, but undoubtedly for different reasons.

"Hello?"

The sound of an unknown woman's voice suddenly filling the kitchen we were in by way of the phone's speaker had

Charlene and I looking at each other in confusion. I quickly grabbed the phone from her hand and turned it so that I could see the woman's face on screen.

"Who are you?" I asked aggressively.

"My name is Erin, I'm your dad's lawyer."

"How did you know he's my...where's Leroy?" I asked, moving past the obvious question to get back to my agenda.

"Hold on," Erin said.

Her face disappeared, but it was clear that she was passing the phone to someone sitting across a restaurant table from her.

"Lia, what's wrong?" Leroy asked, suddenly popping into view.

"That's a dumbass question, Dad. Where the hell are you?"

"I'm out having a late dinner and strategy session with my lawyer. Why? Are you okay?" he asked, sounding genuine enough to make me nauseous.

"I'm FAR from okay, but you would know that if you bothered to do the shit normal fathers do. Just forget it! Enjoy your meal," I said, disconnecting the call before he could spit another lie out of his mouth.

No one had dinner with their fucking lawyer at midnight unless they needed to be believably visible, and Leroy was smart enough to know that. My intuition was spot on, and Leroy's dinner date was all I needed to prove my suspicions.

"You still believe that my father had nothing to do with what went down at that casino?" I asked, looking Charlene squarely in the eyes.

"I-I honestly don't know, Lia. I mean, I don't know of any reason that he would have for targeting the feds, especially with the scrutiny he's under right now."

"That's because you're looking for a LOGICAL reason to murder innocent people, and there isn't one!" I said with mounting frustration.

"Okay, you're right, but still, the best way to understand your father is to make it make sense by the code of the streets. I admit that I'm not from that world, but your dad has that shit in his veins and it guides his decisions, whether good or bad."

"Okay..." I replied slowly, trying to put myself in the mind frame of a crazy street nigga.

"What would make anyone use the feds for target practice, knowing that you're hotter than summer nights sleeping on plastic sheets."

"A threat. They would have to pose some type of threat to him, or someone he loves," I said thoughtfully.

"That makes sense, if it's true. The better question is, why are you trying to make sense out of it at all? It seems to me like you got enough to worry about."

Even though her words were spoken softly, they still packed a punch like dynamite. I didn't know why it was so important for me to prove that my father was the devil, but there was a part of me that NEEDED his evil to make my fucked-up life make sense. Figuring out why would surely make some psychologist rich one day, but today wasn't that day.

"The feds are gonna kill Leroy, or lock him up, which means he's dead regardless. That would mean I'd be just as dead shortly after, and since I'm not ready for that yet, we've gotta figure out how to keep my father alive and free. Agreed?" I asked, extending my hand formally.

"I'd say that's common ground that we can build on."

Once we shook hands, I went back to my phone to see what else I could find out about the casino hit. I sat back down at the table, poring over the articles and videos still being uploaded from multiple news outlets. Whatever threat my father was perceiving didn't jump right out me waving a red flag, which could've meant that the feds were clueless too. The more I read, the more I allowed the hope of the feds' ignorance to grow, but that came to a screeching halt when the names of victims started to surface.

"The feds were in the hotel on a protective detail for some people going into the witness protection program," I said, reading verbatim from the latest ABC news update.

"Okay, well that sounds like either some mob shit or some gang shit, but not some Leroy shit."

"That depends. Correct me if I'm wrong, but isn't one of Leroy's wives named Amelia?" I asked.

The sick look that appeared on Charlene's face said it all, but it didn't make me feel better now to be right. I knew why Leroy had killed all those people, but I also knew that if he was cleaning house then someone was missing.

"We need to find his other wife because she's next, and if the feds realize that, then they'll set Leroy up to trap him. They won't be arresting my dad this time though. They're gonna kill him."

Chapter 11

Leroy

Two days later

"Why do you keep looking out the window, L, when you know the feds are out there?" Erin asked, lighting a cigarette.

"Because I want them to KNOW that I know they're out there, and that I ain't scared of they bitch ass. They pussy!"

"L, calm down and stop waving that fucking gun around," she said, motioning for me to come sit by her on the bed.

It was on the tip of my tongue to unleash a verbal assault on her, but I held back because she wasn't the person I was truly mad at. I was pissed at myself because ultimately, it was my fault that I was in the position of fighting for my life from the shadows. For all the problems I'd anticipated coming with breaking Gini out of prison, I'd still overlooked key things that were now haunting my waking moments. Had I thought about or questioned the loyalty of the women I'd shared my bed with, then I could've eliminated them before the prison break. Just taking care of that one detail was the difference between me pacing the bedroom floor of my lawyer's house, and me sitting on a faraway beach sipping something alcoholic while getting my dick sucked. Leaving the country now wasn't a viable option until all loose ends were tied up, and right now, I had no idea how to make that happen. The shooting exhibition of two days ago was supposed to have given me that peace of mind, like Orajel applied to the gums of a teething toddler, but that didn't happen. Amelia had reportedly been killed in the fire fight, but not Candice. As of now, Candice was a fucking ghost somewhere, and the fact that she was still breathing was haunting me in the worst way.

The sound of a phone ringing stopped my pacing in mid-stride, but once Erin looked at the screen and shook her head, I resumed wearing a pattern in the carpet.

"No one just disappears, Erin. I've paid you a lot of money to find her, so FIND HER," I growled, trying to maintain control of my chaotic emotions.

"Leroy, I'm doing everything I can, and I've called in every favor that's owed to me between here and the Pentagon. Whoever knows where Candice is, is taking that secret to their grave, because NOBODY KNOWS."

"No one just disappears," I repeated, pausing at the bedroom window again to peek through the curtains.

"I agree, but...if I'm not hearing shit, and you're not hearing shit, then MAYBE she's dead and nobody is saying nothing."

This idea caused me to stop looking out the window, and I actually crossed the room and sat beside Erin.

"You think?" I asked, taking the lit cigarette from her and puffing on it.

"I mean, it makes sense when you think about it. Given Amelia's history of mental problems, she was never the reliable one when it came to testifying about your illegal activities. But Candice, she was their ace in the hole, and they would know that her death would damage the case against you beyond repair. The moment you know that, you'd flee the country, legally, and there's not a damn thing they could do about it," she replied.

The logic of what she was saying hit me so hard that I could feel the smile spreading across my face like the first Joker from Batman.

"These sneaky muthafuckas!" I said, chuckling despite my frustration.

I understood that what Erin was saying was purely hypothetical, but it was the feds' style to play mind games like these. It was my job to see through their bullshit though.

"Okay, so how do we verify that?" I asked, passing her the cigarette back and standing back up to resume pacing.

"I can keep checking with my people, and you need to do the same thing now that we've got a different theory to run with."

I pulled my phone out intending to text IG, but it started vibrating in my hand before I could tap out a message. When I saw who was calling, I declined the call and refocused in the task at hand. I sent word to Zuk when I was done with IG, and then I logged into the encrypted network that only my most trusted counterparts had so that I could request their assistance. Being a Ruler opened many doors into the underworld and allowed me to rub shoulders with real bad guys that had a long reach. I kept my legal business out of the shadows, but I couldn't deny how good it felt to wield power like a foreign dictator. I reached out to my man Juan-Carlos, a soldado for the Zeta cartel, and let him know that I needed him to lead a small team to handle whoever had gone after my daughter and killed her wifey instead. I understood all too well the danger in being unfocused when people were gunning for me, but I refused to ignore the fact that my child was in just as much danger right now.

"I need you to send five million dollars apiece to five different offshore accounts. Two million in crypto currency, two million in Mexican pesos, and another million in U.S. cash. No name required for account access; just a secure account number and 16-digit numerical password. Got it?" I asked without looking up from my phone.

"I'm on it. Anything else?"

"Yeah, I need you to make Lia disappear," I replied.

Erin's sudden silence and lack of movement in my peripheral vision made me pause in my text and look up at her. "Did I say something wrong?"

"Y-You wanna make your daughter disappear?" she asked hesitantly.

"Yeah, but not like THAT. I just want her somewhere safe until shit calms down. I want you to charter a private yacht and have it run from Florida up into Quebec. I'll decide where to send her once she reaches Canada."

"Okay, that makes more sense," she said, breathing a sigh of relief.

My phone vibrated insistently in my hand, but I declined the call again and finished up my text messages.

"I'm gonna have some of my Haitian associates trailing the yacht for security purposes, so put another million in my account in Port au Prince," I instructed.

"Not a problem."

It took me ten minutes to communicate with my peoples, mainly because I kept getting interrupted by phone calls, but I still got it done. I sent a text to Charlene letting her know what the next move was and informing her of the role she was playing in it. I was just about to call Lia myself when the sound of knuckles tapping rhythmically on a door froze my fingers.

"Are you expecting someone?" I asked, squeezing the Taurus .380 in my grip a little tighter.

"Relax, Leroy, I ordered us some food," she replied, hopping up off the bed and pulling on a sweatshirt over her boy shorts and sports bra.

I couldn't remember the last time I'd ate, but I knew Erin was doing a good job of taking care of us. She was getting paid well, but I was still appreciative of her because of the inconvenience I'd caused to her life. Not only was she keeping me out of handcuffs, but she was strategizing my next moves with me, AND making sure her family was good from a distance. Even though she didn't say it, I knew it bothered her not to let her kids come back home yet. Her husband thought it was about their failing marriage, and she didn't even have time to assuage his insecurities because she was working for me so hard. That was loyalty. She'd become more than my lawyer because she had stepped into the rarified air of trusted advisor.

Initially, I'd thought that us being locked inside her house together would simply give us a lot of hot and steamy moments of sexual distraction from the real world, but it had been more than that. We'd talked for hours, sharing secrets that not even our spouses were aware of. I didn't like to talk about myself or my past, but Erin made it easy and not at all awkward. If I was considered the Don of this thing of ours, then she was my consiglieri, which made her more than a simple hired mouthpiece. Erin was now a part of this thing of mine.

My phone's vibration brought my focus back to this moment, and I quickly scanned IG's words. It wasn't easy to run a criminal enterprise that dealt primarily in a lot of weapons and a lot of weight when it came to drugs, when you added in the pressures of a fight with the United States government. The knowledge that I could trust and depend on my partners took away the stress that could cripple the infrastructure of our organization, like so many others before us. No matter how big the Nation of Rulers got, or how many members pledged their allegiance, I felt like I could count on IG and Zuk to balance me out. The message I'd just received from IG was instructing me to focus on Lia, while he and Zuk handled all other Ruler business. The Rulers were forever at my disposal, and it felt good to get that reassurance without having to say that I needed it.

"Um, L, we got a slight problem," Erin said.

I looked up from the phone in my hand to ask her what the problem was, but I immediately saw the beautiful chrome 1911 Smith & Wesson .45 pressed to the side of her face. My own pistol was only a few inches away from my fingertips, but reaching for it was the farthest thing from my mind.

"So, is this the reason you kept ignoring my fucking calls, my nigga?" Gini asked, cocking the gun being held to Erin's temple.

"No, I declined your calls because I was working, and I told you that."

"You told me that two goddamn days ago, asshole! I'm your WIFE, Leroy, and that means I get more of an explanation than some random bitch you dump cum in when you feel like it!" she said with open hostility.

"Okay, that's fair, but shooting her ain't the answer. I need her."

"Oh, really? You NEED her? Tell me, Erin, why does my husband NEED you?" Gini asked, grabbing Erin roughly by the back of her neck.

"B-Because I keep him out of jail, and I'm helping to keep y-your family safe," Erin replied shakily.

"Hmm...sounds plausible, but it's hard for me to believe when you two are here all alone, and you're walking around damn near naked," Gini said.

"I-I'm at home, so it wouldn't make sense to have on a business suit," Erin explained.

"It might not make sense, but it would go a long way towards making me feel better. You WANT me to feel better, don't you?" Gini asked sweetly.

"H-Happy wife, happy life," Erin replied, giving me a pleading look with her eyes.

"Gini, put the damn gun down and tell me what you're doing here. There are fucking feds outside, and I doubt they would believe you're a *Walking Dead* cast member," I said, standing up and going to peek out of the window.

"I'm not dumb, Leroy, and I know how to move under the radar without being detected. Plus, I had help," Gini replied, smiling devilishly.

She lowered the gun and pushed Erin back towards the bedroom door like she was giving her the opportunity to run. I had no idea what Erin's intentions were, but as soon as another shadow filled the doorway, I knew that running was never an option.

"Dana, I thought I told you two to remain out of sight in Kentucky," I said, frustrated.

"You also told me to keep her safe. You know your wife better than I do, so you should've known that the moment bodies started dropping and you went radio silent that she was coming out to play. This is on you, L," Dana said.

I wanted to argue, but I couldn't, because I knew she was 100% right. Gini was just as crazy and just as protective as I was, which made her predictably unpredictable.

"Okay, but you two coming down here didn't help," I said, crossing the room to stand in front of Gini.

"I disagree, L. More hands make lighter work, and you know that. We've only been in Virginia a few hours, and we already have info that I'm sure you don't," Dana said confidently.

"Oh yeah? Like what?" I asked skeptically.

"First off, you've got at least one rat in your chapter of the Rulers," Gini stated.

"We're going through confirmation protocols now," Dana added.

"And no, it's not Demon. He's a liability because he has no control of himself when he's sky high on PCP, but as far as we can tell, he hasn't made a statement on the record," Gini said.

I didn't wanna burst her bubble by letting her know that Erin had more or less confirmed the same thing, so I simply listened. "Anything else?" I asked.

"Well, there is one other tiny issue, but it's probably not worth mentioning. What do you think, Gini?" Dana asked.

"I mean, I think it's at least worth a MENTION, but it's better if you spoke on it," Gini replied.

"I guess you're right. Well, word is that IG is planning to oust you from the Nation of Rulers because you're too hotheaded and you're out of control," Dana said.

I took a second to absorb the words without responding, all the while searching my wife's eyes for the truth of what had just been disclosed. "So...I'm a liability?" I asked calmly.

"That's exactly what you are, but IG is too smart to come at you head on, so he's gonna continue to let you put yourself in vulnerable situations that make you act without thinking," Dana said.

"And then he's either gonna kill you, or let you die," Erin mumbled aloud, looking at me with frightened eyes.

It made kind of a sick twisted sense because I was a threat, but I didn't bother focusing on whether or not it made sense. I was only wondering if it was something I would do. Once I was able to answer that question, I knew what to do next, and that made me smile.

"I know that look, Leroy, and it's exactly what I was hoping to see," Gini said, handing me her gun.

Chapter 12

Lia

"Please tell me that you weren't doing the weird shit like watching me sleep," I mumbled, rolling over so that my back was to the woman standing beside my bed.

"No, I wasn't watching you sleep. I just walked in a minute ago. I did stare at you for a few seconds, but that was only because I was trying to figure out how you were gonna take the latest news."

Her words forced me to roll back over so that I could look her in the eyes, because her tone of voice suggested that I wasn't gonna like what she said.

"What is it, Charlene?" I asked, sitting up.

"Well, your father wants you to get out of town for a while."

"Okay...and go where?" I asked, waiting on the other shoe to drop.

"Canada."

My immediate response was quiet contemplation, but I knew that wouldn't last.

"I'm not going to no fucking Canada! Why would he even suggest some dumb shit like that?" I asked, annoyed.

"I don't know, but you know that he has his reasons for what he does. If I was guessing, I'd say that he just wants to keep you safe."

"If that's the case, then we both know that I'm safer when I'm closer to him. I get that he has a lot of associates that he relies on, but I'm not about to put my life in their hands when I don't have to," I said.

"That's understandable, which is probably part of the reason he instructed me to go with you."

This was a move that I should've anticipated, especially since Charlene was the only person I'd been around for the past two days. It was obvious that whatever title the relationship between Charlene and my father fell under, he trusted her, which allowed me to give her the benefit of doubt. I still wasn't sold on the idea of leaving the country though.

"Why Canada though?" I asked, trying to rub the sleep from my eyes.

"I don't know, honestly, but I know that he conducts a lot of business north and south of the U.S. border. Would you prefer to go to Mexico?"

"Absolutely not," I replied, holding up a hand to stop her from going any further.

I hadn't been out of the country, but I'd heard the horror stories about visiting Mexico, and the welcome committees known as the cartels. No doubt, Leroy had probably aligned himself with the criminal elements in both Canada and Mexico, but I had to choose the lesser of two evils in my mind.

"How soon do we leave?" I asked, stretching like a lazy cat.

"As soon as I finish whipping up some breakfast."

"OK, I'ma take a shower," I said, climbing from in between the sheets reluctantly.

Surprisingly, I'd gotten comfortable here in the past 48 hours, but I suspected that a lot of that had to do with accepting the realities of who my father was. That didn't mean I accepted the shit Leroy did, but having no illusions about him and his capabilities made adjusting to my reality a smoother transition.

Charlene and I went our separate ways momentarily, and I embraced the rejuvenation that comes with soap and hot water. Twenty minutes later, I wandered into the kitchen and sat at the table while exchanging texts with Brisha. She'd played another major part in me regaining my sanity over the last couple days. I'd confided in her as much as I could without putting her and her daughter's life in danger, and she'd kept shit 1000 with me. She'd seen a lot of shit in the streets, just like I had, so I valued her opinions and perspective. The friendship I had with her felt almost like a sisterly bond that I would've wished for me and Cyn if she'd been alive. The lesson of how quickly life ended was one I was still trying to accept, and one thing it had taught me was to appreciate the people you love while they're still here. Brisha was someone I loved and appreciated, and that knowledge now had my fingers typing out a different message.

"How are we getting to Canada?" I asked.

"In style, of course. We're gonna hop a flight down to Miami, where we'll meet up with the yacht your father chartered. From there, we sail up the eastern seaboard until we run into those broad-shouldered Mounties in red informs."

"Um, okay, you sound a little thirsty about running into the Canadian police, so get that under control. Secondly, I'm inviting my girl Brisha to come with us," I said nonchalantly.

My revelation was met with silence as she continued to busy herself with breakfast preparations, but I knew she heard me.

"I want someone with me that I know is there JUST for me, and not because my father said so. I appreciate you, Charlene, and I'm not trying to belittle the bonding we've done, I just need a piece from my old life to hang onto," I explained.

"That makes sense, and I don't feel any type of way about you inviting her, but I know Leroy ain't gonna be trying to hear all of this."

"You're probably right, but I don't care. I'm uprooting my life and trusting a man who has given me EVERY REASON in the world not to trust him. I'm not asking for much, Charlene, and I'm not trying to belittle the bond we've made, but I'm asking for your help in making this happen," I replied.

She put a plate of fried eggs, turkey sausage, and toast in front of me before going back to the stove and fixing her own plate. As tempted as I was to fill the silence with a sincere plea of all the reasons my request made sense, I chose to eat my food instead. When my phone vibrated a few minutes later with a message from Brisha, I resisted the urge to open it and continued eating. Charlene joined me at the table, but before she began eating, she pulled a phone from the pocket of her jean shorts and sent a text. Within less than a minute, she got a response back, which made her put her phone down and pick up her fork.

"We leave in two hours, flying private out of Richmond International Airport. Have your girl meet us up there," she said.

"Thank you, Charlene. I really appreciate you."

"You don't gotta thank me, Lia, but you do gotta tell your friend what she's stepping into. She deserves the truth, because this ain't some lavish vacation we're going on. I need you to be REAL clear about the target your girl will be putting on her back, and the backs of the people she loves the most. She's not just coming along as someone to support you. She's picking a side in a war that's going on between your family and the United States government. That is A LOT to digest, sweetheart, but if you care about her, then you'll give her the ugly truth about what coming with us will mean. I'll help you, and I won't even ask for your father's permission, but what I won't do is lie. Leroy us sending us out of town because shit is hot, and getting hotter every second. I have no idea if he was behind the attack at the hotel/casino in Maryland, but let's say for the sake of argument that your intuition is right. That means the blood of MORE law enforcement officials is on Leroy's hands, and you're his daughter, so you will forever inherit his beef. Blood has already been spilled on your doorstep, and it's clear to see how much that still affects you. So, are you telling me that you're ready to take on the responsibility of ANOTHER innocent life just because she was in your circumference? I don't think you are, and I DON'T want that type of pain for you, but... I'll do what you ask if it's what you really want," she said sincerely.

I could feel the silent tears drift from the corner of my eyes and create a slow path down my cheeks. The trembling of my lips made the tears feel like raindrops as they landed on my chin and chest, but they carried with them the weight of life and death. In my heart, I knew that Charlene's words carried no malice or malicious intent, but they were designed and given for the purposes of clarity. The anger I could feel pushing the tears from my eyes faster was held in check because I understood that the pain of loss was the real emotion I wanted to run from. I wouldn't run from it though because if I did that, then that meant Imani died for nothing. I REFUSED to let Imani's life and the love that she'd died for mean nothing. Just like I refused to add Brisha's name to the list of people I'd lost to bullets that didn't belong to them.

I picked up my phone off the table and poured my heart out to Brisha in a text, feeling the weight of truth in every word. When I was done, I wiped my face and finished my food.

"Thank you, Charlene," I said, locking eyes with her so that she would understand all that was behind those words.

"You're welcome. Now let's get the hell out of here."

Chapter 13

Leroy

"Erin, I want you to call Sylvia Burns from NBC News and offer her an exclusive interview with me," I said.

"You sure that's a good idea, L?" Dana asked.

"It's a great idea, because it shows that he ain't trying to hide," Erin said.

"Nobody asked you nothing, bitch, so just take instructions, because that's what you get paid for," Gini said, giving Erin a look that could kill.

"Easy, sweetheart, we're all on the same team," I said, pulling Gini into my arms and giving her a quick kiss on the forehead.

"Leroy, we need to strategize, but I'll make the necessary calls while you handle your...business," Erin said, leaving the room.

I had to tighten my grip on Gini to keep her still in my arms while shaking my head at Dana to discourage her from engaging in the bullshit.

"Whether you like it or not, we ALL need her right now, babe, because she's a topnotch lawyer, and she's loyal," I said, looking down into Gini's eyes.

"Let's ask her husband how loyal she is," Gini replied sarcastically.

"Oh, to be a fly on the wall during THAT conversation!" Dana said, laughing.

"It ain't hard to tell that the bitch ain't got no brakes on her legs, meaning, they spread fast and furious," Gini said.

"L, don't get caught in that lady's Tokyo drift," Dana said, still laughing.

I knew they were trying to get me to take the bait so that the conversation about whether or not I was fucking Erin could take place, but I didn't have time for all of that.

"Dana, I need you to give me the full story on how you know IG is about to turn against me," I said, shifting my attention to the things that actually mattered at the moment.

"One of the ladies in my chapter fucks IG from time to time, but she's loyal to me first and foremost. Apparently, IG instructed her to keep tabs on you and Gini in case you had to be eliminated versus allowing you to be taken into custody. When you disappeared, she let me know about IG, and she told me the parts of his plan that she knew."

"Which is?" I promoted after she paused in speech.

"The plan hadn't always been to kill you; just take back the power you had. The power that IG felt like he gave you. The whole reason he went along with your plan to break your wife out of prison was because it meant that you would have to disappear in the end, leaving him the business of the Rulers," Dana concluded.

"What about Zuk though? Was IG gonna eliminate him too?" Gini asked.

"Nah, because Zuk may be a killer and a businessman, but he's a yes man. Him and IG go WAY back, so he's been his yes man for a long time. I'm the threat because I'm the independent thinker," I replied.

"Exactly! You're the only threat to the empire that IG feels rightfully belongs to him, but he's smart enough to know that an all-out war between you and him would damage the brand and fracture the Nation of Rulers. So, he was content to let the cops kill you, or at least have it look like that, but you're making that impossible. He couldn't let you be arrested because you would still hold your position within the Nation of Rulers, and possibly increase your power because of how much business is conducted behind the wall. His only other option is to paint you as a threat to the Nation of Rulers, and since no man is bigger than the Nation, everyone will be forced to accept it," Dana said dejectedly.

"And what if everyone doesn't accept it? I mean, it's obvious where your loyalty lies," Gini said, turning around so that my arms were still wrapped around her, but she was facing Dana.

"My chapter is loyal to me, and I'm loyal to Leroy because of all that you've done for the Nation since its inception. The dick is good, and we've all been having fun, but it's deeper than that for me. You could've easily got rich and forgot about the rest of us, but you made sure that everybody who wanted to had an opportunity to either break bread with you, or eat off your plate. You've given us complete loyalty, and my chapter isn't the only ones who feel like that. People will follow you, L. It was obvious from the beginning that you, IG, and Zuk were different, and that's why I think it's always been in the backs of people's minds that one day, they'd have to pledge allegiance to ONE king. The shit you're going through with IG is a fight that's as old as time, just like him threatening to kill anyone who doesn't align themselves with him. He's ready for war, even if he has to cheat," Dana replied seriously.

"Cheat? What does that mean?" Gini asked curiously.

"That means this ain't no gentlemen's disagreement or normal power struggle, because IG ain't stupid. He's not underestimating Leroy, so he's already made countermoves against moves that Leroy hasn't even made yet. I don't know what all he's done, but I know he's got more shooters than you right now. Have you heard of the Camero Cartel?" Dana asked.

"The car club?" I asked, confused by the topic change.

"Right, it's KNOWN as a car club for the baddest Camaros across the country...just like the Rulers were known as a bike club in the beginning. By the time the streets really knew what the Nation of Rulers was all about, we had a strangle hold on the country. The Camero Cartel was founded by IG about two years ago, but I'm hearing that their numbers in terms of membership are at least 10,000 strong," Dana explained.

Gini let out a long, soft whistling sound from her mouth that kinda spoke for the both of us. Part of me was surprised, and the other part of me was mad at myself for not seeing this coming. Dana was right when she said that this hostile takeover IG had plotted was a fight that was as old as time itself. There should've always been something in the back of my mind guarding against this possibility. My tunnel vision had my mind wrapped up in Gini, and that had almost cost us both our lives. If I let that happen, then that would mean everything I'd done, all the sacrifices that I'd made, were for nothing. I couldn't live with that, and I wouldn't let that be the case.

"Okay, so now that I know what the play is, it's time to fight back. Doing this interview will show the general public, our allies, and the people who are loyal to us that there's nothing to be worried about legally. Just a whole lot of smoke, and no fire. Going on offense publicly against the feds will show everyone where I'm at with it, while also pushing back against whatever bullshit IG is selling behind closed doors. I'm not gonna tip my hand though, because I don't want him to know that I'm wise to his fuck shit, so we keep him in the loop like we normally would. Dana, that means tell your girl to continue playing her position, and make sure you give her a nice thank you present from me. Cash, cars, jewels, give her whatever she likes, but make sure IG doesn't know where it's coming from. Have her rock him to sleep," I said.

"I got you, L. What's the status on the other situation with Candice? We saw on the news that Amelia is no longer a problem, but nothing was mentioned about your other wife," Dana said.

"Your ex-wife. That's part of what brought us down here," Gini confessed.

"I understand, and we're searching EVERYWHERE for this bitch, but right now, no one knows where she is," I admitted.

Hearing this made Gini step out of my embrace so that she could turn around and face me again.

"Bae, she's the only person who can hurt us when it comes to the story of my escape, so we NEED her dead."

"Why are you telling me this like I don't know, or like I'm not trying to erase her muthafuckin existence?" I asked, becoming annoyed.

"I'm just reminding you of why she has to die. I understand that you have a lot of love for her, but at the end of the day, she doesn't deserve your love or loyalty," Gini said.

"Aye yo, stop playing with me right now because you already KNOW how I move when it comes to betrayal. Loyalty will always mean more to me than love, and if Candice betrayed that loyalty, then there's nothing left to talk about," I stated firmly.

"IF?" Gini asked, raising a quizzical eyebrow.

"Okay, L, Sylvia Burns jumped at the opportunity to do an exclusive, and she'll be here with her crew in an hour," Erin said excitedly, coming back into the room.

"Why the fuck would you have her come HERE to do it?" Gini asked, spinning around so fast to Erin that I thought she was gonna attack instantly.

"Because this is neutral territory that can't be ambushed by anyone who might wanna stop Leroy from going on the air. That includes the feds, and all other potential enemies," Erin replied patiently.

"It does make sense, Gini," Dana said, taking a step in between Erin and my wife.

"It also conveniently gets rid of me too, because there's no way I can be here for the interview when I supposed to be dead," Gini said in a menacing whisper.

I recognized her warning tone, and I knew she was about to pounce on Erin like a seasoned jungle predator. I grabbed Gini's wrist and swiftly pulled her towards me so that I had her undivided attention.

"Listen, I need you focused on the important shit, which is finding Candice. You said that is part of the reason you came down here against my direct orders for you to stay your ass put, right? Then help me by finding her, and put a fucking bullet in her brain. Can you do that for me, bae?" I asked sweetly.

"You know I'll still do anything for you, asshole, but when it's done, we're out of here, and there's NO ROOM for your lawyer on this road trip," Gini replied, giving me a smile that had no warmth in it at all.

I leaned in and kissed her with enough passion to scramble both of our brains while transporting our souls to a different time zone. When I pulled back, I knew with certainty that her ache matched my need, but instead of giving into it, we had to use it as fuel to make it to the other side of these hardships.

"You owe me a proper honeymoon, husband, so you better start thinking about where you're taking me," she whispered.

"I know JUST where I'm gonna take you, baby," I replied, squeezing her juicy ass cheeks in both my palms before letting her go.

"Answer your phone, nigga, or I'm coming back," she warned, kissing me again quickly.

When she stepped away from me, Dana stepped forward and gave me a hug along with a quick peck on the lips.

"I'm gonna sneak the rest of my girls into town just in case some shit pops off. I've got my ears to the streets and I'll keep us safe," Dana vowed.

"Thank you," I replied sincerely.

I could feel the reluctance in both Gini and Dana as they headed out the door, but I also felt their determination. We would come out of this on top, or we'd take the world down with us.

"I'ma grab a quick shower," I said, heading for the master bathroom.

"I'll get us set up in the living room," Erin replied.

I used my time and solitude under the hot water to organize what I needed to say in my mind to make sure that the right emotions lined up with what I intended to project. I knew better than to try and sell my innocence, given my multiple run-ins with the law, but I could always sell the question of reasonable doubt. By the time I met up with Erin in the living room fifteen minutes later, I had my game plan in mind, and all I needed was my audience. I was dressed casually in some blue jeans and a light blue Polo button up, while Erin gave off the wholesome, "money makes me cum" white girl vibes in a burgundy linen pantsuit with matching Gucci heels.

"Very nice," I commented, sitting beside her on the couch.

"Thank you...but I need you to stay focused on the task at hand, because the look in your eyes is making my pussy throb. Business first. We don't have to get into a mud-slinging contest with the feds if we stick to the truth we've been telling. You're still grieving the loss of your wife, you're trying to find forgiveness for her codefendant Pony for orchestrating the horrendous attack on that prison, you don't know why those closest to you are being targeted, and you're begging for an end to the senseless violence. Those are your sticking points, so any question that strays away from the safety of those topics, you make sure to bring back to the focal point. Got it?"

"Your pussy is throbbing though? It gets so much wetter when it does that," I said, smiling fondly over shared memories.

"FOCUS!"

"I'm focused! And I got it. I want you to feel free to interject anytime you want to though, because that's what you get paid for," I said.

"And here I thought you were paying me for this good...cooking I've been providing you with."

We both laughed at the inside joke because only we knew that I'd been eating her pussy every chance I got.

"Stay focused, Erin, because this shit is gonna get worse before it gets better," I warned.

We continued to go over what message we wanted to get out for another half an hour until Sylvia Burns showed up. The entire interview with her took approximately 20-25 minutes, but it went flawlessly in my favor. When it was done, Erin and I decided to have a drink to celebrate, but as soon as I poured the first glass of wine, my phone started ringing. I was expecting Gini or Dana to be on the other end, but it was an ominous surprise instead that left me stuck.

"Who was on the phone?" Erin asked.

"My mom. She said I need to come to her house alone, and that it's a matter of life and death."

Chapter 14

Lia

"You good?" Charlene asked.

"Uh, yeah, I'm-I'm okay. I don't really like flying though," I confessed, smiling sheepishly while fighting to keep my intestines out of my throat.

I could see the sympathy in her eyes as she stared at me from her seat across the aisle. Once the fasten seatbelt light blinked off, she unbuckled her seatbelt and moved to the seat beside me. Other than the pilot and copilot, it was just us and a handful of security people on the Gulfstream IV plane, so there was plenty of room to stretch out and relax. My ass was glued to the seat it was in though, because movement was NOT an option at the moment. Charlene gave my hand a reassuring squeeze before pulling the Apple iPad from its custom case inside the leather pocket of the seats we were in.

"Use this, and find something to occupy your mind. We'll be on the ground in Miami before you know it," she said.

"From your lips to God's ears," I replied, trying to breathe normally as I followed instructions.

I found the Airpods that went to the iPad in the armrest of my seat, and I popped them in so that I could listen to some music. By the time I was halfway through Lil Dirk's album *Almost Healed*, I was more relaxed and back to analyzing what would happen next. I'd never been what one would call innocent, so I didn't hide from the evil in the world like it wasn't there. I may have been naïve to the treacherous ways of some cops, but all I had to do was think about Imani's face to burst that bubble. I was able to accept now that moving forward and surviving this madness meant that more people would die, and I could live with that.

While I had the time on my hands, though, I figured that I should learn as much as I could, so I shifted my focus from music to the news media. I started by reading about the attack on Fluvana Correctional Center. Reading about it this time around without the biased mind of a cop allowed me to see just how tactical and strategic, not to mention audacious, the whole attack had been. I mean, who the fuck uses a predator drone on a civilian target? That was like bringing the United States Army to an after-school fight between third graders! Could love really make someone go to the extremes in the before and after photos of the prison? The better question for me was, would I do all of this to save Imani's life and have her by my side?

As a sworn officer of the law, I knew my answer should've been a firm HELL-THE FUCK-NO. But as a woman still grieving the loss of my soulmate, I finally understood my father on an emotional level. He may have passed along his fucked-up attitude and impatience to me through his DNA, but he also passed along his ability to love beyond the reasoning of mere mortals. I continued to process this revelation on a more subconscious level as I continued to read more about the attack, the aftermath, and ultimately, the manhunt. The evidence pointing towards Gini's codefendant was more solid than what was alleged about my father breaking his wife out, which made me question why that narrative was given so little attention.

The more questions I asked, the more obvious it all became that "they" were after Leroy, so the question became, who were "they"? Leroy had no shortage of enemies when you factored in street beef, old gang connections, business rivals, jealous spouses, etc. The list of muthafuckas that wanted my father's head could be endless, but for me, the starting point was the day he'd killed my sister. I'd thought that killing his own daughter was simply a testament to how callous and coldblooded he was, but if he'd known the things I was just now figuring out, then he would've felt like he had no choice. The cancer of betrayal had spread to his very own child, and Cyn had admitted as much out of her own mouth. She'd actively conspired to kill her own father WITH the police! I couldn't even begin to understand all that he had to have been feeling in that moment, but it made sense that those same demons would be haunting him still. Self-preservation was a law of human nature, but it was the ugly truth that the world wanted to deny. We all wanted to believe in the nobility of falling on your own sword, but you couldn't ignore that your natural instinct was to survive by any means necessary. So had my father murdered his daughter for fun...or did he kill her before she could kill him?

That question was still rattling around my mind when my eyes landed on a news interview my father had given less than two hours ago. The gears immediately shifted in my brain, and I was locked in on the present instead of the past.

"You need to see this," I said, removing an Airpod from my ear and passing it to Charlene.

I positioned the iPad so that we could both see it, and then I pressed play on the interview footage. I'd never seen Leroy in this type of situation, but right off the bat I had to admit that he had the smooth presence of a seasoned politician. It was clear that he had a message to get out, and he was sticking to it. He and his family were the victims here, and all evidence pointed to that except for some alleged anonymous call from Candice. For the first time, he actually explained his polygamous lifestyle, and he didn't badmouth Candice or Amelia. He made his family situation seem normal, and then he played the victim card to the max by speaking about the emotional hardship of losing both Gini and Amelia. It really hit home when he shared that he had no idea where Candice was at the moment, and his fear was for her safety. So, here you had this respectable businessman, who epitomized the definition of an underdog, suffering untold traumatic experiences and losses, but he wasn't even allowed to grieve in peace because law enforcement was on his ass 24/7 instead of finding the people responsible for all the killing going on around him. By the time the interview concluded, and the screen faded to black, all I could do was applaud him in my mind, because I'd never seen a finer production on film in my lifetime.

"The man's a fucking genius," I mumbled in awe.

"You can say that again," Charlene said in agreement.

"Do you think he realizes how crazy it's gonna look when Candice comes out publicly, and accuses him of being full of shit?" I asked.

"After seeing that, do you really think Candice is dumb enough to come out against him publicly? I don't think the cops have anything they can bribe or threaten her with to make her go against Leroy now. I guarantee you that in her mind, that man is as untouchable as God himself."

I thought about what Charlene was saying for a moment, and the longer I thought about it, the more my father's decision to do the interview made sense. Leroy was playing chess on a board that was built with all the components of a Rubix cube, and it took a special type of nigga to be able to do that. He was in a class all by himself, and he was proving that he most definitely was not one to be fucked with or slept on.

"How much of that do you think was his lawyer's idea?" I asked.

"Oh, that was all your father, I'm sure, but his lawyer is smart enough to make all the right plays with what he just gave her. Only an idiot could fuck that masterpiece up."

"What's the next move now?" I asked curiously.

"Only Leroy Bly knows that, sweety, but I can promise you that it'll never be a dull moment. What he did makes sure that you're safe too, just in case he doesn't come out of this on top."

"How do you figure that?" I asked, turning in my seat so that I could face her and not miss a thing.

"The picture he painted will allow you to seek asylum in a foreign country, because it's now public knowledge that your family is being targeted. The death of your younger sister and your stepmother is part of public record, as well as the attack on you that almost got you killed. So when you do surface in Canada, you have cards to play in order to keep yourself safe. On the other side of things, your father's name remains good in the underworld, which allows you to inherit his connections and remain protected."

"Did he tell you all of this?" I asked.

"No, but I've been around him long enough to know how he thinks. No matter what he's doing or what he gets into, he's ALWAYS playing the long game."

"Fucking genius," I said again, shaking my head in astonishment of Leroy's mental dexterity.

If nothing else, I was looking forward to the day when this was all behind us and I could just have conversations with him to absorb the knowledge he'd gathered in his lifetime. I would always be my own person, but it was fascinating to see where I'd come from. I knew all the ways I was like my mom, which was why she'd been my best friend up until she passed away. Seeing the parts of my father that explained the mysteries in me made me feel whole for the first time in my life. I could feel the emotions of this new knowledge threatening to overtake me, but I kept them at bay by refocusing my attention.

"How long before we land in Miami?" I asked.

"It should be about an hour or so."

"I'm gonna try to catch a nap until then," I replied, leaning back in my seat.

She passed me the Airpod back and I put the music back on rotation on the iPad before putting the Airpod in and closing my eyes. My mind stayed stuck on trying to organize and absorb all the information I'd been cycling through for the past few hours, but I needed a break. Some good weed would've made all the difference in the world right now, but I knew I couldn't get that until we got on the yacht. In times of extreme stress, I had learned to meditate in order to clear my mind and reset my energy, so that's what I started doing now. The tempo of the music gave me a focal point, and once I envisioned my mom's face, everything else faded away. Soon I couldn't feel the weight of the pressures I was forced to live with, and it felt like I could breathe a little differently. In this state of calm, I must've nodded off, but as soon as the wheels of the jet touched the earth again, I was jolted back into the present. I felt relief knowing that I had made it safely back from amongst the clouds, and I was actually looking forward to seeing what this yacht life was like. I was just a poor little black girl from Richmond, so cruising the seas on a yacht wasn't a lifestyle I was familiar with. A bitch could learn though!

"Have you been on a yacht before, Charlene? I can swim, so I ain't scared to be on water, but I can't fly, and God didn't intend for me to because he didn't give me wings. That's why I stay away from planes - because it ain't natural," I said, shaking my head as I unbuckled my seatbelt.

When I moved to stand up, Charlene grabbed my wrist tight enough to make me stop moving and look at her. The fear I saw on her face ignited the panic in my stomach.

"What's wrong?" I asked.

She didn't say anything, but I followed her line of sight, and that's when I saw the copilot standing a few feet away holding a pistol equipped with a silencer in each of his hands. My eyes immediately swung to the security team we had with us, but they were frozen in their seats, unable to raise their weapons. To my way of thinking, five people could overtake one person, if we moved together swiftly. Before I could find some way to suggest that, though, the copilot started shooting, and within seconds, the security detail was no more.

"Char-Charlene, what's going on?" I asked, fighting against my rising panic.

Before she could answer, the guns swung back in our direction, and one of them echoed the sound of a dry cough. Charlene's body slumped, and her head fell to the right so that she was looking me right in the eyes. The tiny red hole in between her perfectly manicured eyebrows oozed a thin line of bright blood that signified her life extinguishing. The look in her eyes was one of shock, but it faded fast and settled into the blank nothingness that accompanied a lost life. When both guns suddenly swung in my direction, I felt that same look of shock creeping over my features, but I didn't give into it.

"If you know who my father is, then you'll think twice about it before you pull that trigger," I warned.

"I don't care who you daddy is. This is just business. It's not personal for me."

"I promise you that my father isn't gonna see it that way because I'm his only daughter. It's personal for him, and he's gonna kill everybody you love no matter how old, or how innocent they are," I vowed, remaining calm even in the face of certain death.

"You're just talking shit to save your life, but it ain't gonna work, sweetheart. For what it's worth, though, you should know that I'm getting a million dollars to kill you all," he said, smiling as he took aim at my heart and my face.

"A million? That's all? I can guarantee you five million to let me live, and an extra five million to tell me who sent you. My father's name is Leroy Bly, and if you're really 'bout this life, then you know exactly who he is."

The cockiness that had been etched into the lines of his dark brown face vanished like the sun behind a storm cloud, which told me that I had his attention, at least.

"L-Leroy Bly? As in, the Nation of Rulers?" he asked somewhat fearfully.

"Do you wanna call him, or should I? My dad's really sweet...unless you fuck with what he loves in this world. If you do that, well...you're fucked, and so is your family."

Chapter 15

Leroy

I'd made two slow passes down my mom's block, looking at everything except for her house, trying to find something or someone that didn't belong. After the second pass, I parked Erin's car three blocks to the north of my mom's house, and then I doubled back on foot. The neighborhood I'd bought her a house in was considered upper middle class by most, but in Northern Virginia, the area of Falls Church was only 100k above the poverty line. Still, I would definitely call attention to myself by walking with my gun out the way I wanted to, so I kept it tucked in the front of my jeans, even though I felt extremely vulnerable. I zigzagged back and forth casually between the actual street my mom lived on, and the street behind the house, until I got to her house. With all my efforts at detecting counter surveillance turning up no obvious threats, I crept into her backyard through the door in the ten foot high wooden fence that was reinforced with titanium. It was apparent that she was expecting me because her twin Dobermans, Burt and Ernie, weren't roaming the yard per usual. I quickly crossed the grass, and as soon as my feet hit the brick patio, the flood lights over top of the sliding glass door came on. Out of the shadows came my mom's weathered face, waving me forward while her eyes scanned the night around us.

"Mom, are you okay?" I asked, hurrying to her and giving her a hug.

"I'm fine, son, but come in and I'll explain."

I followed her into the basement, and once I closed the door behind us, the flood lights went off. It took a few seconds for my night vision to adjust, but when it did, I noticed that there was at least one other person in the basement with us.

"Mom, what's going on?" I asked, casually slipping the Taurus .380 from the waist of my jeans into my right hand.

"Alexa, turn on the basement lights. Dim setting," my mom commanded.

The fact that the lighting was dim required little to no adjustment for my eyes when the lights came on, but what I saw still caused rapid blinking on my part.

"What-the-fuck," I whispered in disbelief, automatically raising my pistol in the direction of the perceived threat.

"Leroy, wait!" my mom demanded.

"Mom, move," I said, tightening my grip on the pistol while slipping my finger inside the trigger guard.

"Leroy, you put that goddamn gun down in my house, boy, and don't make me say it again!"

As badly as my trigger finger was itching to get active, I wasn't gonna disrespect my mom, so I lowered the gun to my side.

"Just listen for a minute, son, that's all I'm asking."

I nodded my head, but didn't trust my voice to speak.

"L, I never contacted the Fairfax County police, or anyone, for that matter. I never made a statement about you. I never betrayed you, I swear on my dead son's life," Candice stated passionately.

I still didn't say anything. I just continued staring at her like she was a delicious Thanksgiving turkey in need of carving.

"Leroy, did you hear what she said?"

"Yeah, Mom I heard her. So what?"

"So that means you don't need to kill her, or be looking at her like you intend to kill her, as soon as I'm out of sight," my mom said, moving towards me.

"Why should I believe anything she says?" I asked.

"Because she's your wife, and she's always been loyal to you."

"And because there are bigger secrets between us that would've come out if it was me who betrayed you," Candice stated.

My mind instantly flashed back to the moment we'd first taken our relationship to the physical level, and the consequences for that. I had never forgotten that fateful day, and in the back of my mind I'd been wondering why that truth hadn't come out yet. Candice LITERALLY knew where the body was buried.

"Son I can tell by the look on your face that you're realizing the truth in what Candice is saying. She didn't give me the details because I didn't ask for them, but it's to my understanding that she witnessed you in a kill or be killed situation. Is that true?"

"Yes ma'am," I replied.

"And since you didn't kill Candice after killing someone in front of her, that must mean you trusted her with your life. The fact that she's kept your secret even now should be proof that you can still trust her...but you obviously can't trust everyone around you. I raised you to be a thinking man, son, so THINK, and make it make sense."

My mother's words made me feel like that lucky kid who learned how to survive in these streets while other kids were at home playing with their toys. My education at this woman's feet had been priceless, and it was still paying dividends now. I tucked the pistol back into the waist of my jeans, causing both women to sigh loudly with relief.

"I always told you, since you were just a young'un, that four people can keep a secret if three people are dead. So you know better than to leave witnesses, and the reason she's alive is because you love her enough to trust her. Don't doubt yourself, son, because then others will doubt you."

"I got you, Mom. But Candice, why would someone set you up?" I asked, giving her a quizzical look.

"I don't know, but we've been trying to figure out the same thing. As soon as that bullshit came out on the news, I came straight to your moms, and I've been hiding here ever since."

"Why didn't you call me, Mom?" I asked, frowning as I shifted my attention.

"And lead the cops directly to you or to her? I raised you to be a street nigga, so try to remember that I was in them streets once upon a time too. I know the tricks that them snakes use, so I played it smart."

"Plus we figured that you'd already be out of the country after the shit went down at Fluvana," Candice said.

"I almost was, but the allegations that they said came from you would've made it impossible for us to be forgotten. No point in running then, so I had to clean shit up. By the way, how did Amelia end up in federal custody?"

"I don't know that either, but I think she got tricked into letting them use her as bait to lure you out. She missed you, and that was ALL she would talk about when you didn't come home. It would've been easy for the feds to play on that because she wasn't the sharpest knife in the drawer," Candice replied.

"That's about the only part of this they makes sense, but the question still remains of who was pretending to be you?" I said, looking back at Candice.

"I honestly don't know, L. But you got remember that you got a lot of enemies."

"Especially when it comes to cops," my mom said.

They both had a good point, and so now the question became what was more important: deflecting the attention on me now, or finding out who was behind the setup?

The walls were closing in, and I knew that there weren't many people I could trust at this point, which meant I was looking for a needle in a haystack. That would take time, and buying time meant getting the spotlight off me for a second.

"I'm assuming that you saw my exclusive interview with Sylvia Burns," I said, looking back and forth between both women.

"Damn right, and it was beautiful, son. Doing a follow-up one with Candice would put the icing on the cake."

"My thoughts exactly. Are you up for it, Candice?" I asked.

She crossed the basement to me and stepped into my personal space, forcing me to open my arms to her.

"Leroy, I'll do ANYTHING for you, and you know that. You're still my husband, and the love of my life," she stated genuinely.

I held her for a moment, resting my chin on the top of her head while looking at my mom. The look in my mother's eyes told me that she believed in Candice wholeheartedly, and I had yet to meet a bitch that could pull a fast one on mom dukes.

"Thank you, Mom."

"You're welcome, baby. Now go do what you gotta do to stay alive and out of prison."

"Yes ma'am," I replied, taking Candice's hand and leading her back outside into the night.

"Stay close, and keep your eyes open," I said, moving at a brisk pace.

It took us five minutes to get back to the car, and because Erin was now in the driver's seat like we'd planned, all we had to do was jump in and pull off.

"Leroy, tell me that you didn't just kidnap your estranged wife and make me an unwilling accomplice in the process," Erin said, speeding off down the block.

"No kidnapping; she came willingly. But I'll let her explain," I replied, checking the side mirrors for anything moving in the darkness.

"Oh, I've GOTTA hear this one," Erin said sarcastically.

Candice didn't hesitate to run shit down to her, which included what she knew and what she'd told us in the house. She even complimented both of us on the interview that had aired on television. Erin absorbed the information quietly, not asking a single question, while keeping her eyes on the road in front of her. When Candice was done talking, Erin let the silence hang in the air, but when I glanced at Candice in the backseat, I could tell that she wasn't rattled at all by the mind games.

"Do you believe her, Leroy?" Erin asked finally.

"I do," I replied, still maintaining my vigilance for anyone following us.

"Well, then I guess that's all that matters for now," Erin said.

"What does that mean? For now?" I asked.

"That means that my opinion doesn't matter much in this equation, but L is gonna have to convince Gini and Dana not to shoot you when he ain't looking," Erin replied, smirking.

"Who's Dana?" Candice asked.

"You're fucking funny, Erin," I said, suddenly irritated.

"I'm just speaking the truth, Leroy, and you know it. Don't act like you didn't feel the tension in my house with them there, or like you didn't see the gun Gini put to my head. And I'm just your lawyer! Candice is your wife in practice, has been for years, and her loyalty has been called into question. So do you really think Gini and Dana are gonna trust what Candice says, or are they more likely to take the easy route and blow her fucking brains out?" Erin asked reasonably.

"Who's Dana?" Candice asked again.

I could feel myself getting angrier by the second, but I immediately realized my anger was at the truth of what was being said. I felt like I knew how to handle any woman in any situation, but the deck was stacked against me in this situation. That meant it was stacked against Candice too.

"Leroy?" Candice called out, leaning forward from the backseat.

"What, Candice?"

"Who is Dana?" she asked for the third time.

"Dana is the leader of a chapter in the bike club I'm a part of, and she's based in Kentucky. Right now, she's Gini's personal bodyguard detail."

"Okay…so what aren't you telling me about her?" Candice asked.

"That they're familiar enough with each other to kiss on the lips," Erin mumbled loud enough for everyone to hear.

"I see," Candice replied, sitting back in the seat.

"The look of a petty bitch doesn't really suit you, Erin, so tighten up," I said, shaking my head in annoyance.

No one spoke another word for the hour and a half ride it took to get us back to Erin's house. The feds were still staking out Erin's spot, which meant that Candice and I had to hug the floor board of the car to avoid detection. We stayed that way until we were secure inside the garage, and then we made a mad dash for the house.

"Erin, call Sylvia and find out the best time for her to do her next exclusive with us. I'm gonna work on a hiding spot for Candice until shit blows over," I said, heading for the living room.

"L, you know that I trust you with my life, but I'm only gonna feel safe by your side. Can't I stay with you?" Candice asked, sitting beside me in the couch.

"I hear what you're saying, babe, but I really don't think it's a good idea. I've got people coming for my head from every direction, and they won't hesitate to use you as a pawn to capture me. So I need you to get to safety as soon as we're done with this interview, and just trust me. Okay?"

"Okay, L, I will, but——"

"L, we got another problem," Erin said, rushing into the room.

"What the fuck is it NOW?" I asked, beyond frustrated.

"Sylvia Burns is dead."

Chapter 16

Lia

I could see the lights of Miami International Airport twinkling in the distance, but my mind was a million miles away from here. I'd been sending telepathic distress signals to my father for the last half an hour, but so far, I hadn't seen or felt anything that made me feel like he knew I was in danger. The smell of fresh blood was becoming overwhelming inside the closed capsule of the airplane, and the fact that Charlene was still slumped next to me didn't help the nauseous feeling rolling through my stomach. The voices in my head were screaming louder for me to find a way out of this situation, but I remained calm by reminding myself that Leroy had earned the fear and respect on his name. Ever since I'd let it be known who I was, followed by the proposition to save everyone's lives, the pilot and copilot had been locked in the cockpit. I'd heard raised voices, but I couldn't make out what the argument was about. I didn't get the feeling that the pilot wanted to kill. I thought he just wanted to verify my identity before things got bad. I had no idea what their plan was, but from the looks of the men working on the tarmac, I believed our plane's refueling would be completed in a few minutes. The fact that I was still on the plane signaled that we were returning to the sky in the immediate future. Despite my ambivalence towards flying, that particular fear was at the bottom of the list now that I knew I was in enemy hands.

I'd been trying to figure out which enemy of my father's was the mastermind behind this plan, but there were just too many opps to choose from. The pilot and copilot looked like average black men with slim builds, low cut hair, and nothing to make them stand out or announce that they were with the shit. They didn't give me vibes like they were gang members or part of a street crew, which led me to the conclusion that they were professional hittas. The bad news about that was that it meant there was ice in their veins, which I'd witnessed when the copilot let his gun go off without hesitation. The possible good thing about them being professionals was that this was all business and not personal. That kept the option of negotiations on the table.

I heard the sound of the cockpit door opening seconds before the copilot appeared and walked towards me. Instinctively I wanted to run, but the fact that my wrists and ankles were zip tied would've made running a foolish decision. My police training taught me to show no fear in stressful situations, so I stayed still in my seat, projecting calm and indifference in equal measure.

"I'm still waiting on that phone call," I said.

"There's no need for that right now."

The implied meaning made my stomach drop, making me feel like I was about to become unladylike and shit on myself. As revolting as that thought was, I saved that option in case either one of these niggas tried to rape me. For now though, I kept my cool and kept my head in the game.

"If the call ain't necessary, then what is?" I asked.

"My employer will agree to your terms, but ONLY if you can deliver a guarantee that your father will sit down with them. Just your father, not his associates or his minions. It has to be Leroy Bly himself."

"Why?" I asked curiously.

The way the counteroffer was made gave me police vibes, because why else would you insist on sitting down with a madman? You either wanted to arrest him...or kill him.

"I didn't ask such an unnecessary question. I figured that you not meeting your imminent death was more important."

"Nah, you're right, but I can't speak for my father, and he asks questions when shit doesn't make sense," I replied.

"My advice is that you let HIM ask those questions then. Do we have a deal?"

Part of me knew that Leroy would make the deal in a heartbeat, so I didn't understand my tongue's hesitation to comply with the message my brain was sending it. When the truth finally dawned on me, it surprised me more than witnessing Charlene's execution had. I wanted to protect my father. Never in a million lifetimes could I have seen me feeling a protective inclination towards Leroy Bly, but as I sat here looking into the eyes of this trained killer, I realized that's exactly what I felt. I'd have to wait until later to fully analyze what I was feeling because if I didn't focus, there wasn't gonna be a later.

"I agree to your employer's terms. Now what?" I asked, glancing back out of the window in time to see the fuel truck pull off.

"Now we go meet up with my employer and you have a family reunion with your father."

He moved forward towards me as he pulled a knife from his back pocket. My eyes stayed on the blade, but there was no fear bubbling to the surface because I now knew they still needed me. With that knowledge came a relief, mixed with guilt over Charlene's demise.

"As a show of good faith, I'm gonna cut your hands free, but I'm warning you now that you only get one chance to fuck up and do some dumb shit. I'm authorized to kill you if you present a threat, so I'll be cool as long as you are," he said, slipping the blade in between my palms and resting it on the plastic of the zip tie. He waited for me to nod my head in understanding and agreement, and then my hands were free.

"Let's switch your seat," he said, offering a hand to pull me to my feet.

Once I was standing, he helped me hobble into the aisle, and then two seats forward so that I was as far away from the bodies as I could get. Once I sat down again, he put the seatbelt on me, tucked his knife, and sat down next to me.

"I don't need a babysitter," I said, slightly annoyed because I was helpless.

"Probably not, but you could use a distraction. I saw the look on your face back when we in Virginia, and it's obvious that you ain't a fan of planes. I'm sure that this experience ain't help at all, and since we're about to go right back up, I figured I'd distract you."

The stubborn Taurus in me wanted to argue against wanting or needing anything from this nigga, but I felt the sudden rumble of the plane's engines come alive, and that kept my mouth shut. I closed my eyes and retraced my steps to the land of meditation, seeking and finding my mother's face in the darkness. While this offered some comfort, I could also feel tears stinging my eyes right before their escape from beneath my eyelids and sliding down my face. Charlene had possessed the protective instincts of a mother, and I'd unknowingly been gravitating towards that ever since she'd appeared at my condo and saved my life. True enough, she'd come in the name of my father, but the compassion and empathy she'd displayed came from inside her because that was who she was. I would miss that part of her the most, and that was the source of my tears now. I could feel the plane taxi towards the runway, and when we came to a brief stop, I felt my entire body tighten up in anticipation.

"Here, hit this," he said.

I opened my eyes to see him extending a vape pen my way, which I grabbed like it was a life preserver built to conquer the biggest waves in the ocean. I had just enough time to fill my lungs to maximum capacity before gravity had me pinned to the comfortable leather seat as the plane catapulted down the runway. I held the smoke in until my world tilted backwards, then I exhaled and hit the vape hard all over again. By the time the plane levelled off, I was ridiculously high, and grateful for it.

"Now THAT is what I call a distraction," I said, passing him the vape pen back.

"Absolutely."

We passed the pen back and forth for about ten minutes, and then I knew it was time to stop because I couldn't feel my face.

"W-where are we going?" I asked, fighting against the feeling of sandpaper in my mouth.

"We're headed to North Carolina, and then you're going back to Virginia. You'll call your pops once you hit the state line."

"When do we find out who's behind this play that was made?" I asked, trying to focus on remembering what was important.

"That detail is between you, your father, and my employer. Once I drop you off to my employer, I'm out of this situation."

"You think so? Do you realize that you killed someone my father cared about?" I asked.

"I realize that, but I also know that if everything I've heard about Leroy Bly is true, then he'll understand."

"Understand what, exactly?" I asked.

"That it wasn't personal, and that I was just a tool at the end of the day."

"Ah, and you think that'll make him accept what you've done? Just forgive and forget?" I asked in a sarcastic tone.

"In certain circles, your father's name is highly respected based upon the things he's done, but that respect alone isn't what's kept him alive this long. Not even the fear that people feel because of him is the reason that he's alive and successful. His ability to keep his emotions in check, and separate the business from the personal, is what makes him a true street scholar and survivor. What I did on this plane is nothing your father hasn't done countless times before, and while it WILL make him feel some type of way, I'm sure that he won't waste his time exacting revenge on me. I'm a shooter, but your father will want the person who ultimately pulled the trigger that set these events in motion."

"I hear you, and all of that may be true, but one thing you should know about my father is that he takes his business personal. He may not actively seek you out for payback, but should you ever be in a position to get fucked over by him, I suggest you brace for impact," I replied, shifting my focus to the night sky outside the plane's window.

"Thanks for the warning, but do me a favor though. When you retell this story, I want you to include how I helped you out a little," he said, passing me the vape pen back before he got up.

It was on the tip of my tongue to tell him just how useless that information would be in the end, but I didn't. For that, I was rewarded with some Oreo cookies that he tossed into my lap. I went to work demolishing them absentmindedly because I was already thinking about what would happen when I got back to my father. The silver lining in this situation was that we'd now find out who was behind one of the doors labelled "unknown enemies". I had been in support of taking a long vacation to stay out of harm's way, but this was the SECOND attempt on my life. For me, this shit was personal too. The potent effects of the weed opened my mind to delicious scenarios of revenge, and the longer I let myself play with these ideas, the more I realized the truth of being my father's daughter.

By the time we touched down in North Carolina, I was mentally ready to eat a nigga's heart with just a little salt and pepper added. The snacks on the plane had me mellow enough to cooperate when the copilot cut my remaining zip ties free and escorted me from the plane to the waiting purple Rolls Royce Phantom. There was a slender, attractive, blond-haired, green-eyed white woman wearing a form-fitting black evening dress sitting in the backseat when the car door was opened. My first impression was that she must have been in the wrong place waiting on the wrong plane, but then I spotted the chrome and black Glock .40 resting in her lap comfortably.

"Don't worry, she won't bite," he whispered in my ear, ushering me to the car.

Once I was inside and the door closed behind me, the car began moving, but the privacy partition being up prevented me from seeing the driver.

"I'm sure that you have a number of questions, and we've got a long ride ahead of us, but the only way for the truth to be told is through established trust. Do you agree, Officer Panel?"

"I do," I replied hesitantly, wondering where this conversation was going.

"You have no reason to trust me, nor do I have a reason to trust you, but I'm a woman who does her best to lead by example. I walk my talk."

"Okay. So where's your sign of trust?" I asked, looking pointedly at her and her pistol.

Her response was to pick the gun up from her lap, drop the clip, and eject the bullet from the chamber. She then proceeded to feed the loose bullet back into the clip before slamming the clip into the butt of the gun, and pulling the slide to chamber a round. I was slightly confused by her demonstration, but her next move completely fucked my head up. She handed me the gun.

"Trust is a small word, Officer Panel, but it's a BIG thing because it requires actions. I'm trusting you with my life from this point forward."

Chapter 17

Leroy

"Sylvia's dead? Am I getting blamed for it?" I asked half-jokingly.

"Not that I know of, but apparently she was in a hit-and-run accident on her way home," Erin replied.

"How does this affect whatever you were planning?" Candice asked.

"It just requires some adjusting, that's all. I have to find someone I can trust to tell the rest of our story without painting myself into a corner. Sylvia was more sympathetic to the fact that I'm a grieving widower, so she didn't attack my past like some reporters will. Some muthafuckas will act like they sympathize with me, but they'll really just be waiting on their moment to dig into my past with a snow shovel," I said.

"You already KNOW that I'm not gonna let that happen," Erin said, shaking her head emphatically.

"Well, since we don't want to deal with someone who's unpredictable, why not just do it ourselves?" Candice suggested.

"What do you mean?" Erin asked, intrigued.

"Leroy and I can just do Facebook and Instagram live telling our story, or you can be on there with us asking questions," Candice replied.

My eyes immediately locked with Erin's and I could see that we were on the same page as Candice.

"Genius move, babe, let's do it," I said, impressed by her quick thinking.

"And I think it should be just you two on live together, kinda like a semi-private reunion for people to see," Erin suggested.

"Okay, let's wait until morning since the sun will be up in a little while, and in the meantime, we can still focus on making an escape route for everybody, " I said.

"Everybody can't go, " Erin replied softly.

As soon as I looked into her eyes, I knew that she was referring to herself, and that the idea of us not being around each other was hurting her. Until this moment, it had never crossed my mind that sometime in the near future, I'd have to leave Erin behind, but it was an unavoidable truth. Our lives weren't compatible for a variety of reasons, but the main one that we couldn't get around was that she had children that needed her. Her sons were at a tender age where their mother's love would dictate huge parts of the men they were destined to become. I couldn't rob them of that.

"We'll figure something out. Or maybe one day in the future, the stars will align in a lasting way," I replied, offering hope through shared understanding.

Erin responded with a nod and a sad smile before abruptly leaving the room.

"Well...she's obviously in love with you, so why aren't you letting her come with us?" Candice asked, sitting beside me and searching my face for the truth.

"It's complicated, and right now we don't got the time to worry about adding sister wives to the equation. It's not safe right now either."

Candice put her hand up as a sign of dropping the topic of conversation, which allowed us to get back to the big business.

"Okay, so when we do this Instagram live? We need to——"

My ringing phone interrupted my train of thought, but given the time of night it was, this had to be something important. When I looked at the screen, I recognized the number that Lia and Charlene had called me from before, so I wasted no time answering it.

"Hey Lil one, are you all on the yacht yet?"

"No, Daddy, there's been, uh, there's been a change of plans," Lia replied.

Just her tone of voice alone set off alarm bells throughout my mind, but it was the fact that she'd called me Daddy that told me something was real wrong.

"What's the change of plans, sweetheart?" I asked, keeping my voice calm and carefree.

"Daddy, Charlene...Charlene is gone."

"Gone?" I echoed slowly, hoping I was misunderstanding and trying to stop my mind from racing.

"Yeah...gone. It was just business, and in order for me not to be a part of that business arrangement, I had to make a counter offer."

"What was your offer, and how can I help?" I asked, immediately understanding that she'd been smart enough to use my name as leverage.

"Five million to walk away, with another five million for information on who arranged the original business transaction."

"Done. Where does the money need to be sent to?" I asked, impressed by her poise and negotiating skills under pressure.

"Before we get to that, I need to explain a very important, nonnegotiable stipulation."

I felt my stomach tighten because in the back of my mind I knew this had sounded too easy so far.

"I'm listening, Lil one," I replied.

"The boss wants to sit down with you personally, but it has to be just you. I'll be there, of course. The point of this is to show transparency, and hopefully that can lead to prosperity down the road."

Her words relayed up and down the lanes in my mind, connecting dots along the way until I was looking at the big picture abstractly. Whoever it was that had killed Charlene was willing to let me know who hired them, but they wanted my protection from war, and my resources moving forward. It made sense - IF it was for real.

"Sweetheart, you know that money is no issue, but I don't give out trust or my loyalty, and neither is for sale. Feel me?" I asked, hoping she would catch my meaning.

"Understood, Daddy, but it's me you're trusting. Enough said."

"Okay, sweetheart. How do you wanna play this?" I asked, pushing away the doubts gnawing at me.

"There's a Super 8 motel just across the North Carolina state line off of Route One. Room 1018. Come alone, and don't tell anyone where you're going. Not even your lawyer. I'm sending you the account info for the first five million, and you can send that once we're off the phone. The second five million will be discussed when you get here and hear the whole truth."

"Okay. Stay safe, and I'll see you in a minute. I-I love you, Lia," I said, meaning it now more than ever.

"I love you too."

When she hung up, I still kept the phone pressed to my ear, needing to prolong the connection so that I didn't feel like I'd lost her. While it was true that Lia and I didn't have the best relationship, the reality was that she was the only child I had left. I would protect her at all costs.

"Leroy, what's going on?" Candice asked.

"Nothing, I've just gotta to handle some important business, and I need you to stay here with Erin. No questions asked."

"No questions asked," she replied, nodding her head.

I gave her a quick kiss on the lips before standing up and heading to the bedroom in search of Erin. I found her sitting with her legs crossed on her bed, in front of her MacBook pro, concentrating hard.

"We need to talk real quick," I said, sitting next to her and pushing the tablet out of her reach.

Her preoccupation with whatever was on the screen had been a play to mask the hurt that I was now seeing in her eyes. Even though I'd come in here with the intentions of making excuses for us not working and explaining why I had to leave, I couldn't just ignore her pain. Before I knew it, my mouth was on hers, and we were clinging to each other. Her tongue tasted like fresh grapes, and the way she kissed me back left me feeling drunk off of her. The longer we kissed, the harder it got to breathe, and I didn't care because I only wanted what her lungs were pumping out with every roll of her sultry tongue.

"I have t-to go. Erin, I——"

"Shhh, it won't take long," she whispered, reaching for my zipper on my jeans.

To be safe, I moved the pistol out of my jeans and put it on the bed beside us. Then I let my hands help her out of her linen pants. To my surprise, I came into direct contact with her warm flesh once her pants were gone because she wasn't wearing any panties. She wasted no time taking charge by pushing me down on the bed and straddling me. When she took ahold of my dick, her tongue became more insistent in its invasion of my mouth, and that only made me want her more. The passion and fire of her kisses matched mine, creating a heat that burned white hot instantly. I grabbed her waist to hold her steady as she aligned her body perfectly to begin her slow descent down my shaft, starting with the intense throbbing at the head. The heat from her pussy called to me like a siren, forcing me to pull her downward fast enough to have her moan of pleasurable surprise stuck in her throat. The moment she was fully impaled by me, the clock started, and she rode me like a professional bull rider. Minutes felt like seconds, and with every stroke, her pussy became a vise grip in a waterfall, but I was far from complaining. My energy matched hers, but her ability to squeeze my dick on her way down and on her way back up gave her the advantage for the moment. I could feel her entire body tensing as she started to bounce on me, which told me just how close she was to the end. Quicker than an MMA fighter, I rolled her onto her back, and I had her knees up by her ears when I slammed my dick back inside her. I set a new rhythm like I was running off of fresh batteries, and I pounded her pussy until it gushed for me, making me cum right along with her. I collapsed on top of her, and we both fought for oxygen that seemed to be in short supply while giggling like teenagers.

"I-I needed that," she confessed, wrapping her arms around me.

"Me too," I panted.

"Shit, me three!" Candice said.

I looked up to find Candice leaning against the door jamb, staring at us with pure hunger in her eyes.

"Oh-my-Godddd," Erin whispered with a mortified look on her face.

"It's okay, Candice likes to watch," I said, smiling down at Erin.

"I definitely love a good show, but next time let me get my popcorn," Candice said, giggling as she walked away from the door.

"Did that *really* just happen like that?" Erin asked.

"It did, and it was worth it," I replied, rolling off of her and standing up.

We shared another laugh, but it didn't last long before reality came intruding back into the room. The silence that settled around us as we got dressed was thick, but not awkward. We both knew that I had to go, but neither of us wanted that to be the case.

"Are you coming back?" she asked softly.

"As soon as I can...and definitely before I disappear."

"Disappear without me," she said, looking at me with her heart in her eyes.

"I can't ask you to choose your sons over me...and I can't allow you to do that either. So for now, yeah, it's without you, but I'll stay in touch. We can talk about this later," I said, grabbing the gun off the bed and tucking it back into my jeans.

I kissed her forehead and left before things could get any more emotionally heavy. I avoided another run in with Candice by heading straight to the garage, and hopping on Erin's husband's bike. My instincts were screaming at me to call somebody, even if it was only one person, to let them know where I was going in case shit went sideways. It was uncharacteristic of me to ignore my instincts, but that was exactly what I was gonna do because I wouldn't put Lia's life in danger. She sounded like she had control of the situation, but I knew that was an illusion to keep me calm and compliant. All I knew for sure was that a decision I'd made had cost me my baby girl, and part of my soul, so I damn sure wasn't gonna do that twice. This one was all on me.

Chapter 18

Lia

After so many fucked-up events, including witnessing multiple murders and being kidnapped, coupled with sleep deprivation, it was hard to believe that I wasn't in a stress-induced coma. I was wide awake, and my mind was burning like I'd had cocaine for breakfast mixed with methamphetamine. Even with all of this surprising energy I had, I was still having trouble trying to swallow all the information that my new best friend had been providing me with since we established trust. It wasn't just that the things she'd said were hard to believe. It was the fact that my father had NO IDEA what was going on. Leroy was all-knowing and all-seeing like the Wizard of Oz, but not this time. In this situation, a bitch had dropped a house on him! There was a poetic justice to it all, plus some irony, but I wasn't looking to rub it in his face. There was no doubt that the message ran the risk of getting shot in this situation. All I really wanted was to level the playing field, or even allow my father to regain the upper hand by providing him with the facts that he was missing. My fear was that he wouldn't believe it though. I had no idea what to do if he wouldn't listen.

"My people say that your father is a few minutes away from here. Are you ready?" she asked, sitting down on the queen-sized bed.

I sat down next to her and stared at the door like he was about to walk through it without turning the knob.

"Honestly, I don't know. I don't know what to do if he doesn't believe us. I mean, you have NO IDEA how ruthless this man can be. To say that he and I have a rocky relationship is putting it mildly, and you're a complete fucking stranger, which means he's gonna look at you like you want something. Oh, and you DO want something!"

"What I want is nothing more than what he'd offer me for my loyalty. Men like your father understand that loyalty is everything, like Allah is to Muslims, so he'll respect it. As far as whether or not he'll believe it, I can tell you with complete confidence that he will," she replied.

"How the hell can you be so sure when you've never met my father?" I asked with rising irritation.

"Because all he has to do is look at me."

Given the fact that I was currently looking at her, her response made no fucking sense. She was beautiful, but if she thought that was enough to convince Leroy Bly to abandon the truth he already knew for the ugliness she was alleging, then she was a real-life dumb blond. Knowing my father, he'd shoot this bitch in the face and maybe me right along with her. Before I could let that fear grow into panic the size of an ocean, I heard the familiar sound of a motorcycle engine downshifting.

"He's here," I said softly.

"How do you know?"

"Because I heard a bike. He's alone though because if he'd brought the Nation with him, then I'm sure we would've felt the ground moving," I replied.

I could hear the bike getting closer, and then her phone vibrated. She didn't bother to glance at the text. She reached for her purse instead and pulled out her pistol.

"That's a bad idea, and not a good way to establish trust with him. He's not known for being reasonable with people who pull guns on him, and I was a witness to that," I warned.

"Believe me, I'm nobody's fool," she replied, turning the gun over to me.

We waited in silence for a couple of minutes, and then a knock came at the door.

"You should get that," she said, crossing her legs and putting her hands in plain view on her thighs.

After taking a deep breath, I stood up and crossed the room to the door.

"Hey Dad," I said softly, pulling the door open wide so that he could see into the room.

His eyes moved with the swift precision of a shark seeing under water for miles, and I knew he'd scanned every visible inch of the room in seconds before crossing the threshold.

"Are you okay?" he asked, immediately putting himself between me and her.

"I'm fine, I promise," I said, closing the door.

When I turned back to him and passed him the gun, he looked at me with a baffled expression contorting his features.

"I don't, understand Lia. Were you kidnapped or not?" he asked.

"She was, but we established trust, and now I wish to do the same with you," she said from her spot on the bed.

"I gave you five million reasons to trust me," he replied tightly.

"And I sent it back quicker than you could blink, but I'm sure you didn't check it to see that. You can look now if you like, but I assure you that I'm a woman of my word."

He quickly checked the gun, found it to be locked and loaded, and his confusion gave way to curiosity as he turned to give the woman on the bed his full attention.

"What is this? What the fuck type of game are you playing?" he asked.

I could tell by his grip on the gun and the calmness of his tone that he was moments away from letting the monster inside him out to play. She didn't seem worried though, and that made me question her sanity.

"No games, Leroy, just a business opportunity. I wanna be in business with you."

"You killed a woman I loved AND you kidnapped my child, and you think I'm gonna do business with you? Are you high?" he asked, disbelief mixing with his growing fury.

"In my defense, I didn't know that my target was connected to you, nor did I know that your daughter would be with her. When I found out who your daughter was, I reached out to the person who paid me to kill Charlene, and I let her know about the unexpected development of your daughter. When I was ordered to kill your daughter anyway, I took matters into my own hands and decided it would be better to align myself with you. You're a man of principles. So you see, Leroy, I didn't kidnap your daughter so much as I saved her life, because someone else probably wouldn't have hesitated to kill her."

"Listen to her, Dad. She's telling the truth," I said.

He looked back and forth between her and me, which indicated that he was at least weighing our words, but his grip on the pistol didn't loosen.

"Who sent you?" he asked.

"Dad..." I said, trying to stall for time.

The look he gave me was the nicest "shut the fuck up" I'd ever gotten from someone.

"I asked you a question. Who sent you?" he repeated slowly.

"Virginia Bly sent me," she replied.

"That's bullshit, and we're done," he said, raising the pistol towards her.

"Dad, wait! It's true," I insisted, moving to put myself in between her and him.

"The fuck are you doing, Lia? Get out the damn way," he said loudly.

"Please, Dad, just wait. Kali, tell him all of it," I said, holding up my hands in front of my father.

I didn't understand what happened in the split second it took me to raise my arms up, but suddenly my father was locked in on my face and not the woman behind me.

"Lia, wh-what did you say her name was?" he asked.

"Her name is Kali. Why?"

When his eyes flickered from my face to hers, I could tell that he was seeing through different lenses now. The fury had vanished, but the look of fear that had replaced it was just as alarming for me.

"Why does that name mean something to you, Dad?"

"Because now he knows why I look so familiar to him. He knows my mom," Kali said calmly.

"Who's your mom?" I asked, glancing over my shoulder at her.

"Virginia Bly is her mother," he said softly.

"Bullshit!" I blurted instinctively, looking back and forth between Kali and my dad.

I'd never met Gini, but Kali had confirmed that she was alive and well, and that she'd ordered the hit on Charlene because she was tying up all loose ends connected to her escape. She'd told me that Gini was behind this play, but NOT that Gini was her damn mother.

"You look just like her," he said, in awe and disbelief as his arm suddenly fell to his side from the weight of the gun.

With the gun down, I felt like I could take a step back. That way I could look at the both of them while they talked.

"Why would your mom do this?" he asked with hurt in his voice.

"Charlene knew too much, plus my mom knew you were fucking her *after* she'd specifically told Charlene never to go down that road with you," Kali replied.

"Why would she-why would she tell you to kill my daughter though? I don't understand," he said weakly, taking a seat on the bed.

"Because she wants you all to herself. Eventually, every woman who is close to you will be eliminated until it's just her left, because she refuses to let anyone fuck up what you two have. She doesn't just love you, Leroy. She's obsessed with you," Kali replied.

I could see the pain in his eyes as the truth sank in, but I knew that it wouldn't last long because he would use the anger in order to protect himself. First, he needed the whole truth though.

"Dad... It was-it was Gini who set Candice up."

"Wait, what?" he asked, standing back up quickly.

"It's true Leroy. My mom had already had it planned to eliminate her sister wives by convincing you that they were both the spawn of Judas because she *never* intended to share you with them. It made her sick to her stomach that you were fucking them while she patiently waited for you to break her out, but she kept quiet, waiting, plotting. When IG approached her with the idea of keeping you away from the state of Virginia for good, she knew that she'd have to destroy the comfortable life you'd built here."

"Hold up...when IG approached Gini? Th-they worked together?" he asked, completely dumbfounded.

"Dad..."

I didn't have any words to give him solace or soothe his pain, and I hated that as much as I did the woman who'd caused it. In all the times I'd berated my father, or thought of him as a nothing-ass nigga who was heartless, I'd never thought this side of him existed. His pain was as real as the gun he was holding, and it was just as deadly now too.

"I don't know what plan IG had, but I know that his end goal somehow aligned with my mom's. He paid her $10 million right before she got out, and she gave it to me and my brother Kody to live on while you and her were on the run. I didn't want her money though. I wanted a family. I wanted to learn from you and her because your street savvy, prison knowledge, and business acumen is the needed education to get to generational wealth. When I saw that she was willing to destroy any and everything to further HER agenda, I knew that I had to put myself at your mercy," Kali said.

"Would IG really betray you, Dad? He's one of the founding fathers of the Nation of Rulers, so you two have history."

"And none of that matters because he's greedy. He wants it all," Leroy replied numbly, staring off into space.

I'd never seen the look of utter vulnerability that was on his face and controlling his body language. He truly looked defeated, and that was putting terror in me because I knew how the pendulum could swing wildly.

"Tell me everything you know, Kali," he said, sitting back down beside her.

"I'll do that under one condition. You accept me as I am, and forgive me for what I've done," she replied, holding out her hand.

He studied her for a few seconds before nodding his head and handing her the pistol I'd passed to him. It amazed me that I'd just witnessed a full circle moment, and it made me feel more connected to my father than anything ever had. I sat down on the bed with them and listened as Kali filled in gaps for my father until he had a complete new picture of his wife.

"Does your mom know that you didn't kill Lia?"

"No. I told her I'd handle it, and she's been looking for your other wife Candice. She's somewhat frantic to find her now because she poses the biggest threat of all."

"Who knows where Candice is?" I asked.

"I do," he replied.

"What's the plan, Leroy?" Kali asked.

"It's simple really. Kill IG, kill Gini, take over the world."

Chapter 19

Leroy

I was speeding up the highway at almost 200 mph, but I still couldn't outrun the racing of my mind. Everything in me wanted to deny what I'd heard, but the weight of truth when it's told hits you differently and makes reality undeniable. My world had been turned upside down, and even though I had all the pieces to the puzzle, I still struggled with making it make sense. I'd literally given up everything I knew and built a life around Gini, but that still hadn't been enough, and that made me feel foolish. Utterly and completely foolish. The only way for me to shake that feeling was for me to start righting these wrongs, and that was what I was headed to do. Since I hadn't told anyone where I was going or why, I didn't owe anyone an explanation about my absence. I headed straight for Erin's house, intending to use that as my base of operations, but as soon as I entered her neighborhood, I was overwhelmed by the police presence. I saw them before they saw me, which gave me the few seconds I needed to toss the pistol I'd had on me without stopping the bike. As soon as I stopped at the gate where I could enter the password to get into her gated community, the cops jumped out and grabbed me off the bike.

"I advise you to get your fucking hands off me," I said, fighting the urge inside me to resist with violence.

"Mr. Bly, you're under arrest for grand larceny auto theft because this bike was reported stolen by its owner," a cop informed me.

"That's impossible because my lawyer owns this bike, and she lives right there," I replied, nodding towards the house 500 feet away.

"Tell it to the judge, and put your goddamn hands behind your back," the cop said, yanking my arm behind me.

I wanted to fight so bad that I felt like I was foaming at the mouth, but two things kept my crazy under control. The first thing was that when I looked towards Erin's house, I saw her husband standing out front, smoking a cigarette, watching the whole scene unfold. The second thing I noticed was that the feds were gone from their usual stakeout position. I didn't know how these things added up get, but it was enough for me to chill because I didn't have all the facts. I allowed myself to be taken into custody without further incident, and I kept quiet on my ride to the police station. The routine of booking took less than an hour, and then I was left waiting on a magistrate judge to give me a bond so that I could get out.

It dawned on me as I was sitting in the holding tank that this was nothing more than a colossal waste of time, and that realization left me with a bad feeling. Erin showed up twenty minutes after I was booked, and as soon as she removed her sunglasses, I felt my stomach drop.

"He hit you," I said, making it a statement instead of a question.

"We've got bigger problems. The feds are gonna detain you as soon as you step foot out of here. An anonymous tip led them to one of your food trucks, where they found half a kilo of fentanyl bagged up for distribution, and a rifle used in the shooting attack on the hotel/casino in Maryland."

All I could do was shake my head in disbelief, but my mind was playing defense already. "Just because I own the food trucks don't mean that's my shit," I replied.

"Agreed. I don't know what your employee is saying, but I think this is just a ploy to buy time though. I can think of a few good reasons to have you locked up away from your resources."

"To make me vulnerable," I said.

"To make you vulnerable."

What this really meant was that the hostile takeover had begun, and the deck was being stacked against me.

"Gini is involved in this," I said.

"Wait, what——"

"I don't have time to explain right now, but just know that she can't be trusted and I need you to keep Candice away from her," I said seriously.

A look of stark fright came over Erin's face, and it made me wanna vomit for some unknown reason.

"What's wrong? Erin, what's wrong?

" I-I didn't know, Leroy. When my husband came home unexpectedly, I called Gini to come get Candice and keep her safe. I'm so sorry, but I didn't know what else to do, and I didn't want her to get hurt by him too," she said, crying.

The fear that I felt was as real as the tears sliding down her face, but I fought to keep it down as my mind scrambled to find solutions. I was on the verge of losing everything again, but I wasn't going down without a fight.

"Erin, I need you to pull yourself together and listen to me. I need you to get me OUT of custody. Do whatever, PAY whatever you need to, and get me out!"

"Okay, I'll do everything I can, but then what?"

"Then I'm gonna show you why Ruler is supreme," I replied, already envisioning those that would die by my hands.

"It's not that simple, Leroy, and you need to know that I never meant to hurt anyone. I swear, I never——"

"Erin, what are you talking about?" I asked, confused slightly, and not liking the feeling I was getting from her vibe.

"L, it's complicated - more complicated than you know - because I'm pregnant. And it can't possibly be my husband's baby. It's yours."

To be continued...

Lock Down Publications and Ca$h Presents
Assisted Publishing Packages

Due to an increase in the price of services we have increased our prices. The prices below reflect the price increase as of 11/1/24.

BASIC PACKAGE	UPGRADED PACKAGE
$699	**$1000**
Editing	Typing
Cover Design	Editing
Formatting	Cover Design
	Formatting
	Upload eBooks to Amazon
	Upload Paperback to Amazon
ADVANCE PACKAGE	**LDP SUPREME PACKAGE**
$1,400	**$1,700**
Typing	Typing
Editing (line editing/content)	Editing (line editing/content)
Cover Design	Cover Design
Formatting	Formatting
Copyright Registration	Copyright Registration
Proofreading	Proofreading
Upload eBooks to Amazon	Set up Amazon Account
Upload Paperback to Amazon	Upload eBooks to Amazon
	Upload Paperback to Amazon
	Advertise on LDP's Amazon and Facebook Page

***Other services available upon request.
Additional charges may apply

Lock Down Publications
P.O. Box 944
Stockbridge, GA 30281-9998
Phone: 470 303-9761
Email: lockdownpublications@gmail.com

Submission Guideline

Submit the first three chapters of your completed manuscript to ldpsubmissions@gmail.com. In the subject line add **Your Book's Title**. The manuscript must be in a Word Doc file and sent as an attachment. Document should be in Times New Roman, double spaced, and in size 12 font. Also, provide your synopsis and full contact information. If sending multiple submissions, they must each be in a separate email.

Have a story but no way to send it electronically? You can still submit to LDP/Ca$h Presents. Send in the first three chapters, written or typed, of your completed manuscript to:

LDP: Submissions Dept
P.O. Box 944
Stockbridge, GA 30281-9998

DO NOT send original manuscript. Must be a duplicate.
Provide your synopsis and a cover letter containing your full contact information.

Thanks for considering LDP and Ca$h Presents.

NEW RELEASES

BLOODLINE OF A SAVAGE 1&2
THESE VICIOUS STREETS 1&2
RELENTLESS GOON
RELENTLESS GOON 2
BY PRINCE A. TAUHID

THE BUTTERFLY MAFIA 1-3
BY FUMIYA PAYNE

A THUG'S STREET PRINCESS 1&2
BY MEESHA

CITY OF SMOKE 2
BY MOLOTTI

STEPPERS 1,2&3
THE REAL BADDIES OF CHI-RAQ
BY KING RIO

THE LANE 1&2
BY KEN-KEN SPENCE

THUG OF SPADES 1&2
LOVE IN THE TRENCHES 2
CORNER BOYS
BY COREY ROBINSON

TIL DEATH 3
BY ARYANNA

THE BIRTH OF A GANGSTER 4
BY DELMONT PLAYER

PRODUCT OF THE STREETS 1&2
BY DEMOND "MONEY" ANDERSON

TIL DEATH 2 | ARYANNA

NO TIME FOR ERROR
BY KEESE

MONEY HUNGRY DEMONS
BY TRANAY ADAMS

Coming Soon from Lock Down Publications/Ca$h Presents

IF YOU CROSS ME ONCE 6
ANGEL V
By Anthony Fields

IMMA DIE BOUT MINE 5
By Aryanna

A THUGS STREET PRINCESS 3
By Meesha

PRODUCT OF THE STREETS 3
By Demond Money Anderson

CORNER BOYS 2
By Corey Robinson

THE MURDER QUEENS 6&7
By Michael Gallon

CITY OF SMOKE 3
By Molotti

CONFESSIONS OF A DOPE BOY
By Nicholas Lock

THA TAKEOVER
By Keith Chandler

BETRAYAL OF A G 2
By Ray Vinci

CRIME BOSS
By Playa Ray

Available Now

RESTRAINING ORDER 1 & 2
By **CA$H & Coffee**

LOVE KNOWS NO BOUNDARIES 1-3
By **Coffee**

RAISED AS A GOON I, II, III & IV
BRED BY THE SLUMS I, II, III
BLAST FOR ME I & II
ROTTEN TO THE CORE I II III
A BRONX TALE I, II, III
DUFFLE BAG CARTEL I II III IV V VI
HEARTLESS GOON I II III IV V
A SAVAGE DOPEBOY I II
DRUG LORDS I II III
CUTTHROAT MAFIA I II
KING OF THE TRENCHES
By **Ghost**

LAY IT DOWN I & II
LAST OF A DYING BREED I II
BLOOD STAINS OF A SHOTTA I & II III
By **Jamaica**

LOYAL TO THE GAME I II III
LIFE OF SIN I, II III
By **TJ & Jelissa**

IF LOVING HIM IS WRONG…I & II
LOVE ME EVEN WHEN IT HURTS I II III
By **Jelissa**

PUSH IT TO THE LIMIT
By **Bre' Hayes**

TIL DEATH 2 | ARYANNA

BLOODY COMMAS I & II
SKI MASK CARTEL I, II & III
KING OF NEW YORK I II, III IV V
RISE TO POWER I II III
COKE KINGS I II III IV V
BORN HEARTLESS I II III IV
KING OF THE TRAP I II
By **T.J. Edwards**

WHEN THE STREETS CLAP BACK I & II III
THE HEART OF A SAVAGE I II III IV
MONEY MAFIA I II
LOYAL TO THE SOIL I II III
By **Jibril Williams**

A DISTINGUISHED THUG STOLE MY HEART I II & III
LOVE SHOULDN'T HURT I II III IV
RENEGADE BOYS 1-4
PAID IN KARMA 1-3
SAVAGE STORMS 1-3
AN UNFORESEEN LOVE 1-3
BABY, I'M WINTERTIME COLD 1-3
A THUG'S STREET PRINCESS 1&2
By **Meesha**

A GANGSTER'S CODE 1-3
A GANGSTER'S SYN 1-3
THE SAVAGE LIFE 1-3
CHAINED TO THE STREETS 1-3
BLOOD ON THE MONEY 1-3
A GANGSTA'S PAIN 1-3
BEAUTIFUL LIES AND UGLY TRUTHS
CHURCH IN THESE STREETS
By **J-Blunt**

CUM FOR ME 1-8
An LDP Erotica Collaboration

TIL DEATH 2 | ARYANNA

BLOOD OF A BOSS 1-5
SHADOWS OF THE GAME
TRAP BASTARD
By **Askari**

THE STREETS BLEED MURDER 1-3
THE HEART OF A GANGSTA 1-3
By **Jerry Jackson**

WHEN A GOOD GIRL GOES BAD
By **Adrienne**

THE COST OF LOYALTY 1-3
By **Kweli**

BRIDE OF A HUSTLA 1-3
THE FETTI GIRLS 1-3
CORRUPTED BY A GANGSTA 1-4
BLINDED BY HIS LOVE
THE PRICE YOU PAY FOR LOVE 1-3
DOPE GIRL MAGIC 1-3
By **Destiny Skai**

A KINGPIN'S AMBITION
A KINGPIN'S AMBITION II
I MURDER FOR THE DOUGH
By **Ambitious**

TRUE SAVAGE 1-7
DOPE BOY MAGIC 1-3
MIDNIGHT CARTEL 1-3
CITY OF KINGZ 1&2
NIGHTMARE ON SILENT AVE
THE PLUG OF LIL MEXICO 1&2
CLASSIC CITY
By **Chris Green**

TIL DEATH 2 | ARYANNA

A GANGSTER'S REVENGE 1-4
THE BOSS MAN'S DAUGHTERS 1-5
A SAVAGE LOVE 1&2
BAE BELONGS TO ME 1&2
A HUSTLER'S DECEIT 1-3
WHAT BAD BITCHES DO 1-3
SOUL OF A MONSTER 1-3
KILL ZONE
A DOPE BOY'S QUEEN 1-3
TIL DEATH 1-3
IMMA DIE BOUT MINE 1-4
By **Aryanna**

A DOPEBOY'S PRAYER
By **Eddie "Wolf" Lee**

THE KING CARTEL 1-3
By **Frank Gresham**

THESE NIGGAS AIN'T LOYAL 1-3
By **Nikki Tee**

GANGSTA SHYT 1-3
By **CATO**

THE ULTIMATE BETRAYAL
By **Phoenix**

BOSS'N UP 1-3
By **Royal Nicole**

I LOVE YOU TO DEATH
By **Destiny J**

I RIDE FOR MY HITTA
I STILL RIDE FOR MY HITTA
By **Misty Holt**

LOVE & CHASIN' PAPER
By **Qay Crockett**

TO DIE IN VAIN
SINS OF A HUSTLA
By **ASAD**

BROOKLYN HUSTLAZ
By **Boogsy Morina**

BROOKLYN ON LOCK 1 & 2
By **Sonovia**

GANGSTA CITY
By **Teddy Duke**

A DRUG KING AND HIS DIAMOND 1-3
A DOPEMAN'S RICHES
HER MAN, MINE'S TOO 1&2
CASH MONEY HO'S
THE WIFEY I USED TO BE 1&2
PRETTY GIRLS DO NASTY THINGS
By **Nicole Goosby**

LIPSTICK KILLAH 1-3
CRIME OF PASSION 1-3
FRIEND OR FOE 1-3
By **Mimi**

TRAPHOUSE KING 1-3
KINGPIN KILLAZ 1-3
STREET KINGS 1&2
PAID IN BLOOD 1&2
CARTEL KILLAZ 1-3
DOPE GODS 1&2
By **Hood Rich**

THE STREETS ARE CALLING
By **Duquie Wilson**

STEADY MOBBN' 1-3
THE STREETS STAINED MY SOUL 1-3
By **Marcellus Allen**

WHO SHOT YA 1-3
SON OF A DOPE FIEND 1-4
HEAVEN GOT A GHETTO 1&2
SKI MASK MONEY 1&2
By **Renta**

GORILLAZ IN THE BAY 1-4
TEARS OF A GANGSTA 1/&2
3X KRAZY 1&2
STRAIGHT BEAST MODE 1&2
By **DE'KARI**

TRIGGADALE 1-3
MURDA WAS THE CASE 1-3
By **Elijah R. Freeman**

SLAUGHTER GANG 1-3
RUTHLESS HEART 1-3
By **Willie Slaughter**

GOD BLESS THE TRAPPERS 1-3
THESE SCANDALOUS STREETS 1-3
FEAR MY GANGSTA 1-5
THESE STREETS DON'T LOVE NOBODY 1-2
BURY ME A G 1-5
A GANGSTA'S EMPIRE 1-4
THE DOPEMAN'S BODYGAURD 1&2
THE REALEST KILLAZ 1-3
THE LAST OF THE OGS 1-3
By **Tranay Adams**

MARRIED TO A BOSS 1-3
By **Destiny Skai & Chris Green**

KINGZ OF THE GAME 1-7
CRIME BOSS 1-3
By **Playa Ray**

FUK SHYT
By **Blakk Diamond**

DON'T F#CK WITH MY HEART 1&2
By **Linnea**

ADDICTED TO THE DRAMA 1-3
IN THE ARM OF HIS BOSS
By **Jamila**

LOYALTY AIN'T PROMISED 1&2
By **Keith Williams**

YAYO 1-4
A SHOOTER'S AMBITION 1&2
BRED IN THE GAME
By **S. Allen**

TRAP GOD 1-3
RICH $AVAGE 1-3
MONEY IN THE GRAVE 1-3
CARTEL MONEY
By **Martell Troublesome Bolden**

FOREVER GANGSTA 1&2
GLOCKS ON SATIN SHEETS 1&2
By **Adrian Dulan**

TOE TAGZ 1-4
LEVELS TO THIS SHYT 1&2
IT'S JUST ME AND YOU
By **Ah'Million**

TIL DEATH 2 | ARYANNA

KINGPIN DREAMS 1-3
RAN OFF ON DA PLUG
By **Paper Boi Rari**

THE STREETS MADE ME 1-3
By **Larry D. Wright**

CONFESSIONS OF A GANGSTA 1-4
CONFESSIONS OF A JACKBOY 1-3
CONFESSIONS OF A HITMAN
By **Nicholas Lock**

I'M NOTHING WITHOUT HIS LOVE
SINS OF A THUG
TO THE THUG I LOVED BEFORE
A GANGSTA SAVED XMAS
IN A HUSTLER I TRUST
By **Monet Dragun**

QUIET MONEY 1-3
THUG LIFE 1-3
EXTENDED CLIP 1&2
A GANGSTA'S PARADISE
By **Trai'Quan**

CAUGHT UP IN THE LIFE 1-3
THE STREETS NEVER LET GO 1-3
By **Robert Baptiste**

NEW TO THE GAME 1-3
MONEY, MURDER & MEMORIES 1-3
By **Malik D. Rice**

CREAM 2-3
THE STREETS WILL TALK
By **Yolanda Moore**

THE STREETS WILL NEVER CLOSE 1-3
By **K'ajji**

TIL DEATH 2 | ARYANNA

TORN BETWEEN A GANGSTER AND A GENTLEMAN
By **J-BLUNT & Miss Kim**

LOYALTY IS EVERYTHING 1-3
CITY OF SMOKE 1&2
By **Molotti**

HERE TODAY GONE TOMORROW 1&2
By **Fly Rock**

WOMEN LIE MEN LIE 1-4
FIFTY SHADES OF SNOW 1-3
STACK BEFORE YOU SPLURGE
GIRLS FALL LIKE DOMINOES
NAÏVE TO THE STREETS
By **ROY MILLIGAN**

PILLOW PRINCESS
By **S. Hawkins**

THE BUTTERFLY MAFIA 1-3
SALUTE MY SAVAGERY 1&2
By **Fumiya Payne**

THE LANE 1&2
By Ken-Ken Spence

THE PUSSY TRAP 1-5
By **Nene Capri**

DIRTY DNA
By **Blaque**

SANCTIFIED AND HORNY
by **XTASY**

LIFE OF A SAVAGE 1-4
A GANGSTA'S QUR'AN 1-4
MURDA SEASON 1-3
GANGLAND CARTEL 1-3
CHI'RAQ GANGSTAS 1-4
KILLERS ON ELM STREET 1-3
JACK BOYZ N DA BRONX 1-3
A DOPEBOY'S DREAM 1-3
JACK BOYS VS DOPE BOYS 1-3
COKE GIRLZ
COKE BOYS
SOSA GANG 1&2
BRONX SAVAGES
BODYMORE KINGPINS
BLOOD OF A GOON
By **Romell Tukes**

CONCRETE KILLA 1-3
VICIOUS LOYALTY 1-3
By **Kingpen**

THE ULTIMATE SACRIFICE 1-6
KHADIFI
IF YOU CROSS ME ONCE 1-3
ANGEL 1-4
IN THE BLINK OF AN EYE
By **Anthony Fields**

THE LIFE OF A HOOD STAR
By **Ca$h & Rashia Wilson**

NIGHTMARES OF A HUSTLA 1-3
BLOOD AND GAMES 1&2
By **King Dream**

GHOST MOB
By **Stilloan Robinson**

HARD AND RUTHLESS 1&2
MOB TOWN 251
THE BILLIONAIRE BENTLEYS 1-3
REAL G'S MOVE IN SILENCE
By **Von Diesel**

MOB TIES 1-7
SOUL OF A HUSTLER, HEART OF A KILLER 1-3
GORILLAZ IN THE TRENCHES
By **SayNoMore**

BODYMORE MURDERLAND 1-3
THE BIRTH OF A GANGSTER 1-4
By **Delmont Player**

FOR THE LOVE OF A BOSS 1&2
By **C. D. Blue**

KILLA KOUNTY 1-5
By **Khufu**

MOBBED UP 1-4
THE BRICK MAN 1-5
THE COCAINE PRINCESS 1-10
STEPPERS 1-3
SUPER GREMLIN 1-4
By **King Rio**

MONEY GAME 1&2
By **Smoove Dolla**

A GANGSTA'S KARMA 1-4
By **FLAME**

KING OF THE TRENCHES 1-3
By **GHOST & TRANAY ADAMS**

TIL DEATH 2 | ARYANNA

QUEEN OF THE ZOO 1&2
By **Black Migo**

GRIMEY WAYS 1-3
BETRAYAL OF A G
By **Ray Vinci**

XMAS WITH AN ATL SHOOTER
By **Ca$h & Destiny Skai**

KING KILLA 1&2
By **Vincent "Vitto" Holloway**

BETRAYAL OF A THUG 1&2
By **Fre$h**

THE MURDER QUEENS 1-5
By **Michael Gallon**

FOR THE LOVE OF BLOOD 1-4
By **Jamel Mitchell**

HOOD CONSIGLIERE 1&2
NO TIME FOR ERROR
By **Keese**

PROTÉGÉ OF A LEGEND 1&2
LOVE IN THE TRENCHES 1&2
By **Corey Robinson**

THE PLUG'S RUTHLESS DAUGHTER
By **Tony Daniels**

BORN IN THE GRAVE 1-3
CRIME PAYS
By **Self Made Tay**

MOAN IN MY MOUTH
By **XTASY**

BOOKS BY LDP'S CEO, CA$H

TRUST IN NO MAN
TRUST IN NO MAN 2
TRUST IN NO MAN 3
BONDED BY BLOOD
SHORTY GOT A THUG
THUGS CRY
THUGS CRY 2
THUGS CRY 3
TRUST NO BITCH
TRUST NO BITCH 2
TRUST NO BITCH 3
TIL MY CASKET DROPS
RESTRAINING ORDER
RESTRAINING ORDER 2
IN LOVE WITH A CONVICT
LIFE OF A HOOD STAR
XMAS WITH AN ATL SHOOTER